A CHEERFUL SOUL
and other stories

HERSH DOVID NOMBERG [illegible] 1927) Hersh D[illegible] Mszczonów ([illegible] ket town abou[illegible] Orphaned at a [illegible] his maternal gra[illegible]voutly religious milieu. He began publishing poems and short stories around 1900 in both Yiddish and Hebrew and was considered one of the most influential Yiddish writers of his generation. Nomberg died at the age of 51, having suffered from chronic lung problems for most of his life.

DANIEL KENNEDY is a translator and editor based in France. His first book-length translation, Zalman Shneour's *A Death: Notes of a Suicide*, was published by Wakefield Press in 2019.

SNUGGLY BOOKS

hersh dovid nomberg

A CHEERFUL SOUL

and other stories

translated by
daniel kennedy

THIS IS A SNUGGLY BOOK

ISBN: 978-1-64525-068-5

Contents

A Cheerful Soul / *9*
In the Mountains / *37*
Kol Nidre at the Music Hall / *88*
Am I a Jew or a Pole? / *97*
Ishmael is our Uncle / *107*
By a Lonely Grave / *114*
Shiringer's Demise / *123*
The Rebbe's Grandson / *137*

Translator's Postface / *151*
Glossary / *163*

A CHEERFUL SOUL

and other stories

A Cheerful Soul

I

THE year was 1880 . . . a yeshiva boy from a small Lithuanian town, having caught the bug of apostasy and fled his yeshiva, arrived in Warsaw. The boy's name was Yitskhok Toybkop. At that time he was young, about eighteen years old, and was recognizable—like all those educated in the traditional religious manner—by his hunched, emaciated body, his pale face, his short-sightedness, and a mind that was a confusion of ill-defined desires and notions. By nature he was frivolous and lazy, weak-willed, and lacking in the normal moral instinct of a person who lives among people. But he did possess one virtue which helped him find favor in the eyes of others—his cheerfulness. He was always in joyous, good spirits, ever ready with a joke; he was invariably prepared to make light of himself and adapt to any mood, like a cat that ingratiates itself, asking nothing in return but to be noticed.

The day after his arrival he had already made three friends whom he would slap on the shoulders, laughing encouragingly:

"No need to fret! It'll all be fine! Trust me, it'll all work out . . ."

He also found and changed jobs with the same characteristic recklessness, without undue care or ceremony. He had a sharp mind and was quick to get a handle on any matter, but his old, threadbare clothes always held him back. He was aware of the problem, understanding the effect clothing had on potential employers, and so when he was informed that his help would not be needed he did not lose heart, but stood his ground, took stock of his surroundings, and said with a faint smile:

"You can try me out, what have you got to lose?"

And before the boss could change his mind Yitskhok would rush over to the merchandise, lift up a length of fabric in his hand, and appraise its value with expertise. Then he would scoot over toward the ledger and examine the accounts with such conviction that even the boss was forced to pay attention.

On one particular day Yitskhok crossed paths with a potential employer in a jovial mood—business was booming, and it happened that the man's wife had spared him a nagging the night before. He smiled at the boy's audacity, and agreed to take him on for a trial period: they would see how it went.

During these first days Yitskhok immersed himself in the work with all his faculties, with all his heart, and the boss all but beamed with delight, observing the boy toil with such diligence as if it were his own business. Gushingly, he remarked to his wife:

"Well? Whaddya say to that, Khane? Do I have a nose for these things, or what? I knew right away that he had it in him."

But once a few months had passed Yitskhok grew tired of the whole affair and changed his mind—he would become a bookkeeper instead. And so one morning he approached the boss's desk—enclosed behind a set of railings—and announced:

"Listen, sir, I've been thinking . . ."

"What do you want? Go put the package over there, quickly."

"I'm not going to work here anymore. I don't want to . . ."

The boss was surprised, and before he knew how to react (should he shout, lose his temper, or should he just pretend he hadn't heard?) Yitskhok continued:

"It's no use staring at me like that, sir. I've given the matter some thought and I think I'd prefer to become a bookkeeper. I have no desire to work here anymore—I'm free to leave, am I not?"

"You're free to go to the devil, scoundrel!" the merchant growled, stamping his feet on the floor.

But Yitkhok was not discouraged: he responded coolly, feigning innocence:

"No, boss. I don't want to go to the devil . . . Be so good as to pay me what I'm due for the last eleven days . . ."

Yitskhok knew full well that the boss would not pay up, but the idea of demanding it—in person to begin with, and later, formally, in court—amused him no end. It was an occupation, something to distract himself with and boast about to his friends, who applauded and encouraged him to his face, while ridiculing him behind his back.

"Good man, Toybkop! Shall we go to a restaurant to celebrate? Do you have money?"

That's how they spoke to his face, patting him heartily on the shoulder; behind his back they said:

"What a ragged, delusional buffoon he is: he honestly believes his boss can't do without him!"

⁂

The young man lived like this during a span of three or four years, leaping from one job to another, from one profession to the next, exchanging one boss for another. Meanwhile his head filled up with notions—whole chapters and specific phrases both entire and fragmentary—gleaned from different books, and he made the acquaintance of other similarly minded young men with whom he shared moments of joy and suffering. All the while his unread copy of *The Political Economy* lay open on his desk. Each day he prepared to begin studying the book, but, his mind being entirely unsuited to learning in a systematic, structured manner, the book remained on his desk, and Yitskhok enjoyed nothing of its teachings.

It sometimes happened that as Yitskhok was wandering the streets—aimlessly, in his typical fashion—phrases and half-phrases would dart through his mind, snippets of things he had heard and read, and his brain would feel like an ant-hill, teeming in constant agitation. He would set off with terrible speed, without knowing whither or wherefore . . . then, coming to a standstill, he would lose himself in contemplation and begin performing mental arithmetic: two times two is four, two times four is eight, two times eight is . . . until the numbers became hopelessly tangled, whereupon he would stand there, rigid with pain and think:

"Oh, I still haven't gotten started on *The Political Economy*! What will become of me? . . ."

He would run straight home, open up the book, and begin studying. But it would immediately occur to him that he'd forgotten to buy cigarettes, and so he would go back out onto the streets. Outside the sun shone, the carriages hurtled past, the tram rang its bell, and people rushed and bustled, and among them walked Warsaw's pretty daughters—Yitskhok pushed himself into the throng, and joined the stream of pedestrians.

He encountered an acquaintance on the street who stopped him, asking:

"Toybkop, where are you off to in such a hurry? What's the matter?"

His response was brusque:

"Please, just let me be on my way, I really have no time . . ."

With those words his hands trembled, and his face twisted into such a grimace that the acquaintance did not dare delay him a moment longer and continued on his way.

In this manner Yitskhok Toybkop spent his first years in Warsaw. In the meantime he had found part-time work as a bookkeeper: an hour here, an hour there, running from one place to the next . . . The work was not difficult, and his employers treated him well. He spent the money he earned on various things. He had not yet abandoned his habitual activities and so he spent his spare moments sitting in cafés reading newspapers, or strolling through the streets, meeting up with friends, arguing, debating, and bemoaning the entire capitalist world order.

II

One merchant, for whom Yitskhok worked two hours a day, had a beautiful and modest daughter. She retained an unspoiled naïveté: her face bore the blushings of youth, and a sinuous braid of thick, black hair hung down over her shoulders. She did not so much speak, as broach gentle entreaties. She did not so much walk, as glide by at speed . . . She spent her days at home, having already graduated from gymnasium, under the protection of her parents . . . and she passed the time reading books, knitting, embroidering shirts and other garments. Meanwhile her days were filled with contemplation, and her thoughts were boundless . . .

Once, the young lady came into the shop and let her gaze fall on Yitskhok. He was awestruck: it seemed to him that she possessed an understanding far greater than his own—and his heart was stirred by her beauty.

The days raced by with dizzying speed. Yitskhok took to walking with a more measured gait, his speech and movements became discreet and modest—he was now, by all appearances, a God-fearing man who recognized those things which were higher and loftier than himself. He cherished the times he was free to spend in his room, lounging on his bed, thinking . . .

The yearning in his heart grew ever more intense, and he would often sit for hours at a time listening to every sound, every voice that floated up from the yard. One time, determined to achieve something, he got up and made his way to the water tap. The water flowed, sprinkling drop after drop; he listened to the murmur of the water and thought: I desire nothing, there is nothing at all I desire! . . . He gave a shrug and tightly turned off the tap; he felt quite serene.

On such days he found that the sunlight was much more tolerable, as were the passing figures on the street; even the dark walls of his room smiled down on him. It was only conversations that did not interest him, and he would have preferred his interlocutors to sit quietly so that he could observe them in silence . . . But when night set in, and his room was infiltrated by shadows, he was overcome by a sombre dread. He remembered that he, Yitskhok Toybkop, was nothing but a poor, lonely creature, who possessed nothing to which he felt bound. He thought of the young lady who, at that moment, was no doubt sitting with her parents; her head propped in the palm of her hand so that all one could see was a single cheek, and a diminutive ear . . . he began to long terribly to go to her, but he had no pretext under which to pay a call. This caused him profound anxiety.

The nights were long winter nights. It was snowing; the pavements were damp and the wind was harsh. Pedestrians hurried past, hunched over, eager to get out of the rain and the frost; night watchmen dozed, nestled in their furs; and Toybkop wandered from one street to another until he found himself in an outlying suburb where the wind raged all the stronger, pelting his face and eyes with snow. Suddenly he lifted his gaze and saw that he was wholly blanketed in white. He felt a biting chill in his bones, his feet were soaked through, and he wondered what would become of him.

He began to console himself that tomorrow he would see her, that she would surely pay a visit to the shop . . . though he did not need her, of course, because, after all, he was who he was, and she was who she was, and they didn't really have anything to do with each other anyway. But all these arguments were of no use, and he once again longed to see her, to hear her voice, for her to gaze—but for a moment—on him with her kind, pure eyes.

And he turned to the most popular of his friends, to Mendel, a man of around thirty, if not more. Mendel had a high forehead, and his face possessed a transient ruddiness. His apartment was a kind of sanctuary, offering refuge for all lonely people. They would gather there to smoke, drink tea, or to eat the bread and butter which Mendel always had at the ready. They would also read books, hold discussions, and sing songs until they were prepared to cast off their sorrows and heartache, and let their souls soar. Mendel always had his friends in mind and would look out for them however he could. He took pity on Yitskhok who had so much potential but sabotaged himself at every turn, living however he pleased. Mendel worried about Yitskhok and made sure not to let him out of his sight.

Mendel spotted Yitskhok sitting alone on the bed surrounded by a pile of coats and hats, mute, with a hangdog expression and yearning eyes, his head drooping to one side, refusing all offers of tea, or attempts to talk. Mendel made his way over to the bed. He lifted the coats and hats, put them aside, and sat down next to Yitskhok.

"Why are you so sad?" he asked. "You know, whatever it is, it'll pass, everything eventually passes—have some tea."

Yitskhok was surprised by Mendel's insight; he seemed to know the secrets of Yitskhok's heart without needing to be told.

"Have you ever loved somebody?" Yitskhok asked before falling silent, ashamed as though he had made a grave error.

"I have been in love. But I'll tell you this: if she wants you, marry her. Don't be ashamed—shame is a weakness. If she doesn't—forget about it. Pluck the pain from your heart and it will eventually pass; everything eventually passes, to hell with everything . . ." so Mendel said to him.

"I'd like to see her though, all the same," Yitskhok stammered, instantly feeling his eyes fill with tears; the room was enveloped in a fog. The smoke in the air, the glasses on the table, the bread and butter and the faces of all those present—everything seemed so hazy and Yitskhok felt so alone. He stood up, said goodbye to Mendel and left.

Returning to the streets where the biting wind and snow hounded him, his legs seemed to carry him, unbidden, toward Szaromińska Street, no. 15. He came to a standstill in front of the house and looked up: through a window on the second floor he saw a light burning. The gate was still open; anyone could just walk up the stairs and press the electric doorbell. Oh how beautiful and innocent she was!

"But, I want nothing, there is nothing I desire!" he reminded himself. In his fantasy he vented his rage toward all those people who stood in his way, as if he were a thief or a bandit, or something even worse . . . He was about to turn around and go home, but on the pavement opposite, facing the other way, a lady was walking, and by the lantern-light Yitskhok could make out a long black braid, and by her gait he knew that it was her. His heart pulled him forwards; he followed her until he caught up with her. He turned to face her and saw—it was someone else! He returned home in shame.

III

This is what Yitskhok's apartment looked like:

Walk down Dzika Street as far as the corner and there you will find a gateway cutting through a low building. The floor under the gateway is covered in rotting planks with no shortage of pitfalls; anyone who goes through at night without knowing where the holes are could easily slip. As you come into the yard you'll see a second building with high walls and rows of windows one atop the other. You enter the doorway on the right side of the yard and come to a flight of stairs. The stairwell is narrow and the lanterns are mostly broken so there is not much light, and it's probably better not to lean too much on the banister either as it, too, is broken in many places and you could easily break your neck in the dark. Best stay in the middle of the stairs and keep going up until your questing foot crashes to the floor, meaning that you have run out of steps and reached the first landing. Then you turn and continue climbing the next set of steps. Continue this process ten times until you reach the top. Here you must crouch down a little as the ceiling slopes somewhat. To one side you'll find a doorframe, next to which hangs a skeleton key whose swaying and tapping you could hear as you came up the stairs. Here you'll find an attic room, currently in use as a makeshift enclosure for hens and geese, and just beyond it is the door to Yitskhok's room, where he lives alone.

The room itself is quite large, but there are about six walls and many corners; everything there is diagonal, sloping at different angles and one can discern the architectural ingenuity involved in joining so many slanting walls each trying to evade the other. There are two small windows which open out onto the roof, cutting through the no-man's land between heaven and earth, offering a view of chimneys and the rooftop of the building across the way. Beside one window stands a small wooden table, on which you'll find: a smoke-blackened lamp, with a cracked rim; a selection of Russian newspapers and books, such as *Life*, *God's World*, *On the Development of Political Foundations* and *The Political Economy*; empty matchboxes; a cardboard shirt-collar with an old, wrinkled shirt-front; a glass of cold tea dregs, crumbs of sugar and bread, and some left-over butter smeared on a piece of paper . . .

By the table are two chairs. One is so crooked you'll need to hang on for dear life to avoid sliding off, while the other is completely intact and ranks as one of Yitkhok's most handsome pieces of furniture. This chair is generally not free, however, as it usually plays host to a pile of clean clothes: shirts, underwear, etc. The iron cot, with a lone pillow and a blanket, spans the distance between two walls, leaving a long triangle of free space behind it, in the corner of which lies the pile of dirty clothes which often serves as a hiding place for certain forbidden pamphlets . . .

Otherwise there is a small kerosene stove for boiling water, a plate, a bottle for kerosene, two more glasses that sit in the corner, and a broom which stands by the door, embarrassed by how seldom it sees any use. The whole floor is littered with scraps of paper, used matches and cigarette butts, which come to life whenever Yitskhok strides across the room: they spring forth and are tossed against each other whereupon they tumble and recombine into fresh and novel formations

This is the room Yitskhok came home to that night.

It was eight in the evening and Yitskhok was in the habit of returning home late, having little choice in the matter . . .

He lit the lamp, picked up a book and began to read, but his head was swarming with impressions: a gaze, delicate lips, a sweet imploring voice, the dangling braid of hair, smooth cheeks, small ears and it all filled his soul to the very brim, catching in his throat.

He stood there, and looked around—at the empty and desolate walls, at his lonely bed, at the darkness beyond the window—and remembered that he would have to sit there for another four or five hours, all alone. A sinister dread came over him. He began pacing to and fro across the room, his feet displacing the scraps of paper and cigarette butts on the floor. From the corridor he heard the geese honking and flapping against the wall . . . and suddenly an idea swam to the surface of his mind, an idea compelling enough to drive away his melancholy and lift his spirits. He ran quickly out of the room.

IV

In the second floor corridor Yitskhok stood in front of a door, impassively reading over the words on the brass plate, gleaming in the light of the gas-lantern:

He felt more at ease now, though exhausted. His heart was pounding, his brow was drenched in sweat. "I came in such a hurry!" he thought, marveling at the speed with which he'd covered the distance from his room to there. It felt as though he had not come under his own steam, but rather a wind had carried him there, as he could not remember the details of the walk. His thoughts and feelings were like those of one sobering up from a bout of intoxication.

He began to inspect his clothes: the ends of his trousers were torn and muddy, and had accumulated clumps of debris. He attempted to straighten himself out, brushing off the dirt and smoothing out the wrinkles on his trousers until they looked half-way presentable. He then straightened out his hat, which was damp and creased, and ran his fingers through his beard which for two weeks had seen no sign of a razor. He was ready to ring the doorbell.

In fact there were two doorbells. One, a simple bell operated by pulling a cord, and the other, an electric one that rang the instant you placed your finger on a button. Yitskhok pondered which bell to ring, and so he stood there, rehearsing what he was going to say while grimacing and biting his lip.

"Herr Keyserowitz, I would like to earn some money . . ."

In his mind he had prepared a whole oration, along with an unwieldy smile, which he believed suited the words. He rang the electric bell. He stiffened his resolve, stood up ramrod-straight and waited.

He heard faint, muffled footsteps and the door opened. By the threshold, so close to Yitskhok, she stood—it was her, the beautiful young lady with all her naïveté and charm, so delicate and gentle, as light as a childhood dream . . . He took a step forward and she shut the door behind him.

"Is Herr Keyserowitz at home?" Yitskhok asked.

"My father? I'll go and check." she stammered.

She turned and went into the next room; Yitskhok watched her undulating braid, which reached down to the shiny, black ribbon around her waist and it felt as though all the rooms were permeated by her beauty.

She soon returned and enquired:

"You would like to see my father? You work for him, if I am not mistaken?"

"There's a matter I'd like to discuss," Yitskhok responded with a smile, feeling that he had regained his composure. " . . . I wanted to propose a match." A cautious smile hid behind his eyes and lips. He waited for a moment before adding:

"I wonder if I could speak openly to the mademoiselle? You won't be offended? I wanted to speak to your father about the possibility of your engagement . . ."

"*My* engagement?" she whispered, her face flushing. She also has an urge to smile, but felt that a smile would be misplaced. She stood aside and went through into the large room. He followed her and she pointed him toward the right door whereupon Yitskhok entered the office of Herr Keyserowitz.

Herr Keyserowitz was an unremarkable looking man, dressed half in the traditional, half in the modern style; he had narrow eyes, and his beard and eyebrows were black. He sat at his desk opposite a thin, lively man, clean-shaven and bespectacled. Judging by his unbroken speech and rapid gestures—constantly removing notes from a briefcase—he must have been an agent. Yitskhok closed the door behind himself and waited.

Keyserowitz's head turned, dragging his small body with it. He strained his eyes to look:

"Panie, eh," he said, frowning and squinting, ". . . Toybkof? Take a seat."

He turned his attention back to the agent. The agent also turned a curious eye toward Yitskhok, but, determining that Yitskhok was no business man, he turned back and resumed his speech. He spoke and spoke ceaselessly at an outlandish tempo while Keyserowitz listened calmly and impassively, only occasionally lifting his hand slowly to utter a few unclear syllables: a mark of his disaccord, whereupon the agent would gird his loins once more and increase the torrent of verbiage, catching Keyserowitz by the hand as though to prevent him from escaping . . .

Half an hour passed in this fashion and all the while Yitskhok sat there, his heart bursting with longing for the soul separated from his by just one wall, longing for the translucent face and the delightful movements, the lowered eyes. He grew bored, and frightened. He fidgeted on the chair and began to regret everything: the deed he had come to perform, the marriage proposal he was about to suggest, his entire conduct, and his whole life . . .

Finally the agent left. Keyserowitz rose to his feet and turned to Yitskhok.

"What news with you, Panie Toybkop? Eh?"

"News?" answered Yitskhok, "I have no news to tell—where would I get news? But there is a matter that I would . . . I would like to earn some money from you, Herr Keyserowitz . . ."

And a smile moved across Yitskhok's lips, a smile that could be interpreted in various ways—First interpretation: "I, the speaker, am a nobody, an utter simpleton." Second interpretation: "I am indeed on a higher level than his lordship, I know what goes on deep in his heart. The third: "I am mocking you." And there were countless other ways one could have interpreted that smile too . . .

Keyserowitz approached Yitskhok, looked him over and said:

"You want to earn money? Oho. Good. Of course, everyone has to earn a little money."

"Herr Keyserowitz, I would like to propose a match for your daughter. I've heard that you are on the lookout for suitors, and so I thought I would step in, perhaps you would agree and there would be some money in it for me? Everyone would gain something."

"Aha, indeed, naturally, go on," Keyserowitz said.

"Naturally you are acquainted with Mr. Shoyber who works for the D. Brothers?"

"The D. Brothers," Keyserowitz nodded.

"He earns a hundred and twenty rubles a month, is cultivated, and . . . in short, is an industrious man: he is a traveling salesman, speaks Russian, Polish . . ."

"Ah yes, him!" Keyserowitz remembered, "I once had some business with the man, continue . . ."

Yitskhok became braver and continued his praise—The potential suitor came from a respectable family, was well-mannered, decent in his affairs, did not waste money, and so on. His words seemed to be getting through to Keyserowitz who invited Yitskhok to sit closer by the desk, where Keyserowitz listened intently.

"It's true I am looking for someone. Someone—I mean not just anybody of course. He has to be a real *somebody*, a decent man. And this fellow doesn't sound bad at all!

There's something to talk about. Let's have some tea."

They agreed that Yitskhok would return the following morning accompanied by Shoyber and they would introduce him to Keyserowitz's daughter so that she could get to know him . . .

"You understand me, Panie Toybkop," Keyserowitz explained, "we live in a changed world. They should get to know each other first. My daughter has graduated from gymnasium and she deserves to have a modern fiancé. Don't think that she is a libertine. God forbid, far from it, but these days a young couple should get to know each other first."

On his way out Yitkhok once again saw the girl. Her hair was no longer in order, her braid had been undone; she sat by the table, her head propped in her hands, and did not even turn to look at him . . .

"Good evening," Yitskhok said. But he did not receive an answer.

1910

In the Mountains

I

WHENEVER I hear the words *youth* or *health* I picture Sonia—a young painter I met several years ago in Munich—as vividly as if she were standing before me. Judging by her appearance few would guess that she belonged to the race of artists. A round face with full, rosy cheeks; a hale body, athletic and strong; eyes full of energy and life: in short, a woman of passion and strength, lacking so much as a hint of feminine weakness. How such a creature could wield a paintbrush with such tenderness and fantasy was a mystery to many. Her whole being struck one single note, drowning out all others: her health, her budding youthful physique, charged with vitality. It was only later that I noticed hints of originality in her features: a raw, untamed wildness that sometimes flashed, fast as lightning, across her face as she spoke; and in the angular corners of her splendid brow I discerned much innate refinement. In all she was no older than twenty but possessed considerable talent. The professors sang her praises. Her paintings depicting cattle, flocks of sheep, the silent sea and the southern sky (her father was a Jewish landowner in southern Russia) were executed with care and originality. On top of all this she was a free-spirit, open-hearted sometimes to the point of vulgarity; she adored all manner of sport, movement, light, and gaiety. Two weeks after our first meeting I had already completely fallen for her. And she was fond of me too, more than any of her other acquaintances at any rate.

We did not ask much of each other; we did not take our relationship too seriously and so we lived happily. She did not go in much for fragility or tenderness; she did not wish to be passive, even in matters of love. Silent yearnings or trembling feelings were alien to Sonia: her passions assailed her like a storm wind. Sometimes, as we walked together on the street, she would take my hand and squeeze it tightly, nestling up to me like a child. On other occasions, as we sat together in her apartment late at night, I witnessed her agitation. I saw how the flash of wildness ran over her face, then she would stand up suddenly and demand that I leave.

"Get out of here! Go home! And don't come back tomorrow either!" She would say this with resolve.

Ignoring all protest on my part she would grant me one parting kiss before pushing me toward the door.

"Go! I'll come to you, if I feel like it. But for now, get out this minute!

Around that same time, I was beginning to take an interest in a certain acquaintance of mine—a Jewish student from Russia who had half-assimilated himself here in Germany. Schwarzwald was his name. He was intelligent, very cultivated, but with a weak, lyrical character: poor, rejected and lonely. A broken man. I attempted to paint his portrait, laboring long and hard on it, but I was entirely unable to capture his essence, that which had caught my interest in the first place. His was a gaunt, sickly face with sunken cheeks and a prominent jaw. He had a long aquiline nose, which in itself was not ugly or caricatural but in contrast with his haggard face it seemed to protrude excessively. And yet there was something deeply sympathetic about his face that attracted one to it—that elusive *something* I was unable to capture, unable to paint. In the lines of his jaw, and the folds around his mouth, there lay a strange submissiveness, a helplessness, a hopelessness . . . No I'm not expressing myself properly, all of that lay in his deep, gray sorrowful eyes—the lines of his face contained something else—a sanctity? No, not that either. A stillness, a calmness—the tranquility of a dead face. It was enough for him to close his eyes, and bow his head a little, for any trace of life or animation to vanish, and it would appear as though what we had before us was the head of a cadaver. His whole being seemed to be bent double with suffering, but even his pain was no longer alive: it lay dead, frozen onto his face. Despite all this, one could not discern the faintest shadow of bitterness; no trace of malice or irony was to be found on his face.

I mentioned him to Sonia and she came to my studio to catch a glimpse of him, as though he were some sort of exotic tribesman from America. She arrived as Schwartzwald was posing for me, and immediately she began to inspect him from every angle—from up close, from far away, in profile—unceremoniously, without addressing a single word to him. I felt almost embarrassed. I knew Schwarzwald well, knew the inner pride he maintained despite his kind nature. But Sonia soon composed herself and attempted to justify her behavior.

"Forgive me, Herr Schwarzwald," she said, "for allowing myself to examine you like this. It's what we artists are like: for us nothing exists except form and color. Is that not true?"

I noticed that she'd made quite an impression on my acquaintance. It never occurred to him to be offended, and he responded affably.

"True, of course."

"And here, you see, I'm always arguing with him," she said pointing in my direction. "He says that seeing form and color is not enough—that one must also feel the *soul* of the thing. That's what you say, isn't it? I've never seen a soul. I don't even know what the word is supposed to mean—how am I supposed to *feel* it? What do you think, Mr. Schwarzwald? I've been told you're an intelligent man with a good understanding of art."

"Oh!"exclaimed Schwarzwald, "I'm no artist, merely a student of philosophy. All I can do is philosophize about art—for an artist that sort of thing is entirely superfluous."

"That's what I like to hear; I say precisely the same thing myself! I don't want to *know,* I want to see and paint. Seeing and painting is all that matters."

I interrupt to protest:

"But one must also have a heart, and feelings. One needs to have a relationship with the thing one is painting, a spiritual perspective . . ."

And we began bickering in our usual manner. Schwarzwald remained silent. He wasn't so much listening to the young painter as watching her—she who was so enamoured of form and color. In the end he took her side.

"You're doubly wrong!" he said to me. "Your first error is that you debate at all—leave that to us philosophers, your job is to paint. Secondly, to see something, to truly see it with an artist's eye is the same thing as seeing it with heart and feeling and a spiritual perspective and however else you want to call it . . . you're arguing over semantics!"

In the end we all stood back to appraise my work. None of us liked it. I was the most disappointed of all. The following morning I started again from scratch but I could not finish. I began a third attempt with a different pose, but nothing came of that either.

II

Sonia often visited me while I worked. Afterwards Schwarzwald would accompany me to Sonia's place where we would while away the evenings together. They were tedious evenings, passing slowly and gloomily, leaving behind a feeling of dissatisfaction in our hearts like an oppressive unfamiliar worry. Schwarzwald would sit in silence. We were too self-conscious to speak in front of him. How could we philosophize as we used to when our ideas did not interest him? He had heard them all a thousand times before. Idle chit-chat was likewise impossible; his presence cast a dark shadow over our moods. His very being radiated hopelessness, the desolate sorrows of worlds long destroyed. In his presence it seemed as though only one thing could be contemplated or discussed—death.

During those long evenings of tedium, I scrutinized his face closely, studying every line, each and every wrinkle, every gesture and movement. Observing his every expression in this manner I soon discovered a terrible secret: the poor man deeply worshiped Sonia. He devoured her with his eyes; he had fallen in love with her, senselessly in love, with the full force of his capacity for hopelessness! Whenever she spoke, or moved closer to him, his face took on a strange new expression. It seemed as though the frozen agony on his face had started to thaw, coming alive, telling terrible, heart-breaking stories, and begging, begging . . . oh, how repulsive his face was in those moments.

How ungainly, how sickly-weak, how pitiful and foolish. On several occasions I could no longer stand to look at him and had to cover my eyes. As for Sonia, she was bored. Such evenings left her sombre and apathetic, yet she never made any attempt to avoid him. On the contrary: she always asked him to come, and was reproachful if he allowed several days to pass without paying a visit.

"Tell me," she asked after he had gone, "what does a person like that live for?"

I said nothing, but she importuned me as though I was at fault, as though it were *my* life.

"He doesn't believe in anything, doesn't love anything, doesn't hope for anything; he's entirely apathetic! Nothing interests him: not books, not people, not art—nothing. So how on earth does he live?"

"He lives because he lives. What do *I* live for? what do *you* live for?"

"What do I live for? For the love of art!"

She spoke those words with such pride and confidence that she could have convinced the greatest skeptic. It was the artist in her that spoke, glinting in her eyes.

"Perhaps he does love somebody. You can never tell," I remarked sardonically.

She seemed to grasp what I was alluding to and, in lieu of a response, a satisfied smile played across her lips.

This was her way of bringing a conversation to an end: with a special smile that lit up her whole face, hinting at a deep feeling of happiness and boundless self-love.

Evening after evening went by in this manner.

She was bored by him and yet she toyed with him. She complained to me about the "Black Shadow"—that's what she called him—that cast a strange melancholy onto her soul, yet she continued to invite him over and never stopped goading him on. She would take him by the hand, and ask him to touch the muscles in her arm, to see how strong she was, all the while leaning her young, fresh body toward him, her chest thrust forward. Like a child, the poor man obeyed her every command.

Meanwhile I continued to labor over his portrait despite the mounting suspicion that nothing would come of it. And when I could no longer stand my work along came Sonia in a white fur hat, with glowing cheeks and a pair of ice-skates clinking in her hands, flooding the room with all the freshness and beauty of the bright frosty winter's morning that she herself so strongly resembled. Schwarzwald stood up and greeted her with a merry boldness that was entirely out of character. This was one of those unhealthy euphoric spells that befell him from time to time, like a sudden flicker of a flame. He was then alert and exuberant, like a new man.

"Any progress with the portrait?" Sonia asked.

"Nothing will come of it," I answered.

"Let me have a try," she said. "Sit down, Schwarzwald."

She threw off her coat, took up a pencil, and began to sketch a few lines. She soon grew bored, however, and put aside the work. It's not for me." she said.

"No, please. Draw me, I beg you," Schwarzwald pleaded with her. "You must draw me, I just know that you'll be able to do it. Only you can succeed."

"How do you know that?" she asked unceremoniously.

"I know. I'm sure of it; I can feel it. Please! Draw me."

Pleading and persuasion were not in Schwarzwald's nature and sounded so strange on his lips. I cringed to hear him speak in such a tone.

"Leave me in peace!" Sonia responded. "I am incapable of drawing a face such as yours."

"Why?"

"Because it is not beautiful."

Schwarzwald was taken aback by the bluntness of her words, though he appeared to accept that there was truth in them. How many times had he complained to me of his unsightly outward form? The color drained from his face and his mood changed abruptly. He became gloomy and silent, the frozen pain on his face lay dead once more.

We all felt uncomfortable. As Schwarzwald was leaving, Sonia begged him to pay her a visit the following day. She smiled, making eyes at him as though nothing had changed.

III

Coming to wake me, a god left Olympus,
and bid me arise from sleep,
Shamed and slumbering human, arise,
who hath fled from life—awake!
Where is thy youth?—Forgotten.

Where is thy happiness?—It has flown away.
Where is thy hope?—Dead.
Arise, Arise, for thou didst dream an idle dream.

I have come, sorrowful wretch, from a far-away land! From a land where the well-spring of life murmured for generations gone by; from the land of eternal beauty I have come to rouse thee—Arise!

A new day will be born in the East. A new light pours o'er valleys and mountains, o'er forest and field, and with gold-ringed clouds crawls o'er the sky, to announce the good news to the world, and to thee—the idle dream is over—Arise!

The morning air is full of fresh odors, mild winds do blow to quicken every flower, every blade of grass. "Awake, Arise!"

Voices of pure bells tremble in the air; and the new brightness grows ever brighter, and the sun rends its purple veil asunder and emerges, fresh and young and new-born. Wake up sleeping human, awaken thine evil and good feelings, wake thy hope—The time hath come, Arise!
What awakens within thee?—Thy dormant youth.
What flows in thy blood?—Craving for happiness and love.
What dazzles thine eyes?—Thy rousèd hope.
Arise!
The black veil has been pulled from thine eyes and the shadow of death hath been chased away. I pour life and desire into thy limbs—I, the god of love!
Arise!

This was the poem, composed in German hexameter and entitled "The Rising," that Schwarzwald brought me, handing it to me with an air of embarrassment.

"Here, read this over, if it isn't too boring for you," he said.

I read it through and looked at him uncertainty.

"Well, what are you looking at me like that for, do you like the poem?"

"Yes, certainly, very classical, fitting for a philosopher, but . . . well, don't take this the wrong way, but you're in love, aren't you?"

Slightly ashamed, he responded with a smile.

"And what if I am?

"What indeed."

He began pacing across the room. It was clear he wanted to discuss something with me. He was in one of his elated moods; his eyes sparkled.

He turned to me abruptly.

"You know of course who it is I'm in love with, don't you?"

"Naturally. At any rate, she is worthy of it."

"Are you an honest man? You wouldn't tell a lie?"

"By all accounts."

"In that case I want you to tell me the truth—are you jealous? I want to know."

"I'm not sure where you would get that idea, Schwarzwald. It would never occur to me to be jealous, I assure you. My relationship with Sonia is very casual. We are two free-spirits. And what's more . . . how should I put this . . ."

I very almost finished my thought: that I felt secure in Sonia's healthy instinct.

But I stopped myself in time, leaving the words unspoken. Schwarzwald did not seem to notice; he was more concerned with unburdening his own heart:

"You're a good man. I'm truly fond of you. And you know . . . I'm in love! Head over heels in love. I've never felt this way before. I cannot think about anything, cannot talk about anything but her. I'm not capable of living without the thought of her, without it my blood will refuse to flow through my veins . . . You'll say that I'm a fool, that I'm mad, but you don't understand, you cannot understand. You don't know what it's like to live an apathetic, lifeless existence without joy, without delight, without hope, without happiness. Am I deluding myself? So be it! I want nothing more than to be a fool. I want to cling to my illusions. I can no longer tolerate my nihilism—one can only live for so long in such a state . . .

He then took leave of me and went home. His face had seemed troubled, his eyes had burned with an unhealthy fire, and all in all he'd given me the impression that he had gone half-mad.

"Looks like congratulations are due for your new conquest," I said to Sonia later that same day. "Schwarzwald is madly in love with you. Here, read this!"

I handed her the poem Schwarzwald had given me. She read it and concluded that she did not like it.

"Just like that you have conquered a new heart; you should be proud." I said with annoyance.

"And I suppose you're jealous? I was under the impression that I was still a free woman."

"What? Are you not ashamed to say such things? Me, jealous? Of whom?"

She laughed and asked, "He's really in love with me?"

"Madly in love."

She did not respond. But a smile appeared on her lips. There it was again—Sonia's smile.

IV

Half way through that glorious winter Sonia had the idea of going hiking in the mountains, and she convinced Schwarzwald and me to come along with her. We dressed up like tourists, warm and light. Sonia was dressed all in white. She wore a knitted jacket, which lent her healthy body a certain charm, and a white fur hat, which sat coquettishly on her head.

Schwarzwald and I wore short, warm leather jackets, large hobnailed boots, long socks that reached over our knees, and Tyrolean caps with a feather on the side. This sporty ensemble, it must be said, did not really suit Schwarzwald's figure, but he took a childlike satisfaction in the outfit. As I had already noticed, he had changed quite a lot in recent days, becoming sometimes manically energetic while at other times falling into a heavy sadness, giving me the impression that he was an unstable melancholic.

We left Munich in the middle of the night, and arrived at Kufstein a few hours before dawn. Kufstein is a small town in North Tyrol, just on the other side of the Bavarian border, surrounded on all sides by mountains: the Bavarian highlands on one side, and on the other side a whole chain of mountains, collectively known as the Kaiser Mountains, which stand like outposts of the mighty alps. We waited in a restaurant for the sun to come up, whereupon we donned our backpacks and set off, walking sticks in hand.

The town lay shrouded in a thick fog; we couldn't even see the buildings on the other side of the square. This was no ordinary fog, but a thick cloud that poured into the valley from the mountains, looming oppressively over everything, and over us. Figures roamed through the clouds like shadows, their movements seeming otherworldly. Sometimes they would vanish from view only to reappear again a moment later, emerging from the gray sea. Of the newly risen sun there was no trace, and alongside the fog, there was also a slippery frost to contend with. Tired and drowsy, we clung together like a flock of frightened sheep in order to prevent each other from slipping.

We walked in silence, deep down regretting that we had listened to Sonia's crazy idea of going into the mountains in the very midst of winter. Sonia herself, usually so cheerful and energetic, also walked in silence, penitent. No doubt she felt that she had indeed sinned—against me especially. If only we had been alone, but no, she had insisted Schwarzwald come with us.

Despite the fog we made our way to the mountain, and began our ascent. For quite a distance we walked, slowly dragging our feet, groggy and lost in our thoughts. When we reached a height of about 2,000/2,500 meters we saw that the fog had vanished. The air was clear and limpid, though we could still not see much around us: we found ourselves surrounded by trees. The path itself cut its way through thick banks of snow on either side. We could only see a few meters in front of us, as the path wound its way—like all mountain paths—leading us in zigzags.

"Well, how are you feeling, *Gnädiges Fräulein*?" I asked Sonia with a hint of bitterness.

"Very well, *Gnädiger Herr,*" she answered coldly.

"Schwarzwald! Where are you?" she turned to our acquaintance, who was still trailing behind us.

"Coming right away!" he shouted back, breaking into trot to catch up with us.

There is nothing worse, while hiking in the mountains, than changing the tempo of one's pace; one tires more quickly that way. I mentioned this to him but he responded with bluster.

"It doesn't matter, I won't get tired."

And in that moment he truly did seem to have grown younger, his voice sounded stronger, more confident—*The god from Olympus has risen*, I thought to myself . . .

As we continued we began to notice dappled pools of light, tracing patterns on the snow amongst the shadows of the trees. Looking upward, we could make out patches of blue sky through the tangle of branches. Everything suddenly became more convivial. We had long ceased to feel the cold in our bodies, warmed as we were by our own movements. Encouraged, we quickened our pace. The path before us twisted and turned like a snake: the same trodden snow in the middle, and the same frozen snow on the sides, and so on without end. The flecks of light and the blue sky sometimes disappeared entirely. We had been walking for over an hour and the path to the mountain peak was estimated to take about four or five hours—unless we stopped for a rest at the inn that lay at the halfway point, in which case the prospect seemed all the more tedious.

But just then our path emerged from the woods, and we found ourselves suddenly awash in warm light, a dazzling, crystal-clear whiteness hit our eyes from every direction. We had unexpectedly entered a bright new world. We looked up—the sky was clear, sparkling and gleaming like smooth glass. All around us—a world of snow. Everything shone, from below, from above, from the abyss; from the deep plains to the peak of the mountains that surrounded us, everything sparkled. The eye bathed in the light, as if in a spring of pure delight—to behold it was almost painful, enough to drive one to tears. We stood still in wonder and enchantment.

Our path now followed the very edge of the mountain, and the surrounding area for several miles around revealed itself before our eyes. At the foot of the mountain lay the Inn valley, bordered on the far side by high mountains. The river Inn snaked its way through the valley, looking like a thin, gray strip on the backdrop of white snow. In one corner of the valley we could make out the houses of Kufstein, thrown together in a pile, as tiny as houses of cards. A thin cloud, its tendrils brushing up against the nearby mountain, still hung over the houses: the same fog we had met as we were leaving the town.

And around us stood the mountains. Of different heights, and different shapes, they pressed themselves against one another, or crept up over each other's backs. Some of them were formidable with their sharp jagged outlines; while others appeared as though poured into soft forms like a woman's bosom. The whole formation gleamed and sparkled, blanketed in snow and bathed in light. To one side we could see a small group of mountains, with three high, wild peaks, stretching upward into the heavens. They shook the snow from themselves, revealing bare gray stoney bodies, looking for all the world like accursed giants; wicked and terrible, they seemed ready to kill, were they not riveted to the spot by some even mightier force . . . We recognized them as the "Wild Kaiser"—a range notorious in Tyrol, with many frightful tales tied to their name.

"Oh, how beautiful!" we cried out, all together.

Schwarzwald all but wept with rapture, his eyes were damp and his gaunt face radiated bliss, like the face of a saint.

"I'll tell you this, my dear friends!" he cried out. "It's worth living and suffering a hundred years to see this spectacle, however briefly. Just look at that ravine! Just imagine throwing yourself down there, to die on the spot and be covered in the same snow as everything all around . . ."

We looked downward in the direction he'd pointed, and saw a deep chasm just beyond the snowbank—something was stirring down there, murmuring in its depths: a mountain stream, just out of sight. We could only discern a thin plume of vapor, slowly leaking from hidden cracks and caverns.

The sun was above us now: it must have been about midday. The path was not very steep there but continued in a straight line leading toward a second incline. We strolled at a leisurely pace, tapping our long sticks in the snow, exchanging only the most necessary words.

Sonia too was silent. It was only in her eyes that I could read the impression the views made on her. Her usually cheerful, energetic expression had vanished, and I noticed, perhaps for the first time, a deep yearning in her eyes, a gentle melancholy. She turned to Schwarzwald and offered him her arm. They walked together, while I followed a little behind. After about another half an hour we arrived at the inn which stood halfway up the mountain. We ordered a round of mulled-wine, dropped our frozen backpacks into a pile on the floor, and relaxed. There was a steady stream of guests arriving from both directions. Those fine, heroic Tyroleans greeted us as good friends and spoke to us in their German dialect, which we understood only with difficulty. Each of them seemed to think it his duty to sit down next to Sonia and tell her how beautiful she was.

"*A kräftig mad'l,* quite a lass," one of them whispered in my ear, winking at me, while nodding his blond-bearded, patriarchal head.

Sonia took it all in her stride, and smiled. She simply smiled.

V

"Onward march!" Sonia shouted, jumping to her feet. We stood up too, readying ourselves to set off on our way again.

The bright, happy sun once again shone over our heads, the shimmering whiteness intoxicating the soul. We no longer felt any fatigue, despite the hours of trekking behind us. Our feet seemed to move of their own accord. We inhaled the light, crystal-pure mountain air, and each breath granted an unfamiliar pleasure. We saw once again the three peaks of the Wild Kaiser, its chasms, valleys, and plains blanketed in virgin snow. The stoney ridge of the Wild Kaiser seemed to smoke; a minuscule cloud crawled along, appearing for all the world like a helpless creature, clambering towards some hidden nest in the mountain peaks. The higher we climbed the more peaks came into view, new valleys and new plains, and far, far in the shimmering distance, stood the Alps leaning against the very sky. Sometimes their silhouettes stood out sharply to the eye, sometimes they looked like a host of clouds, bathed in sunlight; they seemed to move. The Inn valley, the river, the town and its surroundings had vanished entirely from view. We felt separated from the humdrum, gray world we had left behind. Three people, alone amid the mountains and boulders, clouds and snow. The unusual liveliness building up inside us sought an outlet, and so we started to sing, to run, to shout. An echo answered us from all sides.

Schwarzwald was intoxicated most of all. His merriness expressed itself in primitive ways. He screamed in a quivering voice, summoning the echo. He sang and dashed about, his face flushed, his eyes glinting like a madman's. Toward Sonia he felt uninhibited, like a brother. He took her by the hand, straightened the hat on her head and did not leave her side for a single minute. Sonia played along, only occasionally glancing in my direction as if to say: "You see what it means to be in love? This is how I want it; this is how I should be loved . . ."

We began to encounter other hikers on the path; some of them were coming down from the summit, while others had come up from below, catching up with us. But because the path was one of sharp twists and turns it wasn't long before we found ourselves alone again. Suddenly a strange cry rang out and we couldn't make out if it was coming from behind us or ahead of us:

"Hop-hop! Hop-hop!"

The echo answered from all sides. And before we had a chance to figure out what was happening, a small sled came sliding towards us with great haste down the steep path and sitting upon it was a man, red-faced and drenched in sweat . . . he pulled on the reins just in time and turned the sled to the side, colliding with the snowbank. The man fell off, rolling several times over the path, and then, standing up as though nothing had happened, he turned to us with a reproachful half-smile:

"You have to stand aside! I shouted 'hop-hop!' or didn't you hear me?"

We offered our apologies and checked to see if he'd been injured. He explained that falling was not the dangerous part; the worst that could happen is you might roll as far as the next bend in the road before getting up, unharmed. It's all part of a special alpine sport called "bobsledding," you see? We had heard the word before, but this was the first time we had witnessed it, and we were quite shocked to see how violently the sled turned at breakneck speed. A moment later and the man had returned to his vehicle and slid off down the hill, disappearing from sight. Soon we saw more bobsledders arrive, and we stood by the side of the road to let them through. They flew past like lightning, leaving us reeling. On some of the sleds there were couples; we witnessed a healthy, red-faced Tyrolean girl in national costume, gripping tightly onto the gentleman steering the sled. The girl shifted her weight backward in order to keep balance and from time to time she plunged a foot into the snow to better take the bends. We had barely a moment to enjoy this cheerful spectacle before they disappeared from view.

And then once again we heard a "hop-hop! hop-hop!" coming from above.

"Can we try it on the way down?" Sonia turned to me.

"You wouldn't be afraid?" I asked.

"Where would you get that idea?"

"And what if you fall?"

"I'll get up again."

I praised her for her bravery and she was pleased with the compliment. She gave me a warm glance, clasped my hand tightly and said:

"I must get back to my cavalier. The "Black Shadow" will miss me. There's something so fascinating about him today. Does that make you jealous?"

"No."

"We'll come down together on the same sled, you and me?"

"If you like."

"Good." She squeezed my hand again and went back to join Schwarzwald.

Another hiker caught up with us—the tall, broad Tyrolean with the patriarchal face and the blond beard,—the very same who had whispered "*a kräftig Mad'l*" into my ear. He slowed his pace for our benefit and we talked—about the mountains, about the avalanches, about Alpine life. He was proud of his homeland and of its natural beauty. He told us that at the inn further up, a celebration had been arranged by a local club. He himself was a member of this club. There certainly wouldn't be anywhere for us to sleep up there: we would have to come back down that evening, by bobsled, to the other inn below. He explained that there was no danger of getting lost: the path always lay between two banks of snow. There was just one place, where the snow was lower and the path passed directly in front of the chasm, where one needed to be careful. He advised us to traverse that part on foot, because a few years ago an accident had occurred there.

Soon we reached the spot in question. The Tyrolean brushed aside some snow from the wall, and we saw a stone bearing the name of the unfortunate who had fallen into the valley below, and the date on which the event had taken place.

We looked down, and the mighty depths gave us a rush of vertigo. Some instinctive terror befell our souls gazing into that abyss—so deep one could barely discern the whiteness of the snow on the valley floor.

This was the "Devil's Grotto" as it was called on our maps: a terrible, barren hollow, practically unreachable.

"There's a way down from the other side of the mountain," the Tyrolean explained, "but that pass is closed now. You can only go there in the summer, and even then, in broad daylight, it's still dark down there."

"How deep is it?" one of us asked.

Instead of answering the Tyrolean picked up a handful of snow, pressed it into a ball, and threw it into the chasm. We strained our ears and several seconds passed before we heard the slap of snow hitting the bottom.

"Over two hundred meters," he answered.

We were starting to feel cold; an icy wind was blowing, and the sky became dull and dark. It looked as though the sun had lost its nerve and was now trembling with fear. From far off we heard strange sporadic cracking noises, like the sound of trees being felled. Sometimes we imagined a storm was coming, and that the noise was thunder claps rolled through the mountains. Soon we were in complete darkness, and the wind hurled frozen snow into our faces: it was an avalanche passing over the Wild Kaiser. The wind had carried a mass of snow in our direction, blocking out the sun.

"It'll be over soon," the Tyrolean consoled us. "Avalanches don't come down this way."

He began to tell us what to do in the event of an avalanche: "You have to do like this . . ."

He stretched his arms up into the air and mimicked large strides with his legs.

"It's like swimming . . ." he said, "you have to swim your way out of the snow." Having imparted this advice he then bid us farewell. Soon he was out of sight. We felt uneasy, half expecting an avalanche to come and bury us alive. How frightful it must be to be gradually smothered under a mass of white snow. A slow terrible death. It's not unheard of for waylayed tourists to suffer such a fate that can last up to twenty-four hours. "Why did he leave us?" we wondered. No doubt he wanted to save himself, knowing that we'd slow him down! *It's like swimming* . . . the words echoed in our thoughts, and the snow, which not long before had enchanted us with its clarity, refreshed the eye and flooded our souls with wonder—that same snow now appeared as a terrible gray, stormy mass, whose sole purpose was destruction.

Our fear did not last long however. The blizzard was behind us now. Barely ten minutes had passed and once again the sky cleared up, shimmering like polished glass. The sun bathed us in its warm rays, causing the snow underfoot to sparkle and glisten. Our high spirits returned with doubled strength. Our delight soon gave way to pure intoxication. We threw ourselves down onto the snow in the middle of the road, and sat there singing a song that echoed all around. Far from the world below, we felt as though we'd been released from its chains. Schwarzwald started using the informal pronoun "*du,*" and both of us lost all inhibitions toward Sonia. We kissed her, lifting her up under the arms like a pair of satyrs cavorting with a nymph in a Rubens painting. She tore herself from our grip and pulled us forward, suddenly launching herself down onto the snow, laughing so loud it echoed around us like thunder.

The stony neck of the Wild Kaiser was still smoking: the cloud had grown ever larger, and had begun to settle down over the peaks that by now lay behind us. By the time we arrived at our destination—the inn situated at a height of 2,500 meters—a thick cloud filled the valley below, covering peak and plain alike. Only above us were the mountains still visible, sparkling in their snowy coats, bathed in the benign glow of the evening sun.

VI

By the time we had rested, and had something to eat, a sweet weariness had spread through our limbs. Like everything else around us, tiredness felt somehow different there. It did not encourage sleep, but wakefulness, a yearning for sights, sounds and movement. But something had changed in Schwarzwald. He sank into one of his heavy moods. He sat there wordlessly, head in hand, all his weight resting on one elbow, his dark eyes glazed over. Sonia and I decided to leave him there, and go outside to watch the sunset.

The cloud below us was turning red. In places the sun broke through forming strips of purple. Soon the purple turned scarlet, and it looked as though the thick mass had caught fire. Closer to us, the cloud was darker, bathed in pale violet. The temperature was dropping quickly. All these changes came about with an unusual speed. Colors played across the clouds, changing from one moment to the next, becoming now darker, now brighter. Shadows of pink, red, purple and violet drifted to and fro, chasing and pushing each other aside. The sun sank, dipping below the surface of the clouds as though it wished to bathe in the sea of colors. Here and there the mountains poked through, taciturn, earnest witnesses to a solemn ritual. Their peaks were still brightly lit, and they seemed to marvel at the clouds, born of their crevices, which had emerged into the world, growing and spreading until they swallowed up the sun.

Soon the last rays of light were gone, yet the mountain peaks remained illuminated. The clouds below had grown dark, and in the spot where the sun had been a moment ago, a flame burned, as though fueled by hidden coals.

We stood together in silence, Sonia and I. She rested her head on my shoulder. It had turned frosty-cold and gloomy once the colors had been extinguished, and the cloud turned a shade of glaucous black. Only a few pink shadows remained on the peaks. Behind us lay the round summit of our mountain. We looked around, unable to believe our own eyes. Everything was blanketed in a varicolored coat of indescribable hues: a dreamscape of blended violet-pink, soft and tender. Glowing spires as far as the eye could see that seemed to sing a gentle melody, a song that trembled in the air and vanished.

Sonia snuggled up close to me; I felt her bosom pushing against my body. She wrapped her arm around my neck and kissed me. There were people standing next to us—they did not smile, nor did we feel shame. The gesture felt as simple and natural as the world around us. That's when we noticed Schwarzwald; he was standing there staring at us, shivering with cold . . . how terrible his face looked at that moment, with his aquiline nose protruding so incongruously. It was the face you'd see upon gazing one last time at a man who awaited death's gentle release. I let go of Sonia and approached him.

"Are you cold?" I asked.

He said nothing.

"We'll soon get warmed up. There's nowhere for us to sleep up here."

"Yes," he mumbled indistinctly.

We hired two sleds: one for Schwarzwald, the other for Sonia and me. Sonia was in a good mood; she slapped me on the shoulders, laughing and horsing around. She joked with Schwarzwald, all the while calling him "Black Shadow."

"You're not afraid, Black Shadow, are you?"

"I don't know."

"You're turning into a boring fool."

He did not answer, but she refused to leave him alone. She was in high spirits, and was excited about the journey that still lay before us: a midnight sled ride, flying downhill at great speed, by my side, like the Tyrolean couple we'd seen earlier. She was in the mood for talking, with an urge to tease Schwarzwald.

"You cold there, Schwarzwald?" she asked him.

"A little."

"And what will you do if you fall?"

He fell silent again.

She sat down on the sled behind me. I turned around and placed a finger over her lips: "Shhh, that's enough!" I whispered to her.

She laughed aloud.

"Let's get moving," I commanded. "Schwarzwald, try not to follow us too closely. If we fall, pull on the brakes, or else you'll fall on top of us. Okay, one, two, three, march!"

Sonia held me tightly and the sled slowly began to move.

"Watch out!" I called back to Schwarzwald. "When the path goes right, brake with your right foot, and when it goes left, brake with your left."

"And if you fall don't forget to get up again," Sonia added.

By now it was completely dark; the black sky was strewn with shining stars.

The mountains, decked in gray coats, seemed to slumber. But the stars shone and twinkled, and followed us along the way. We moved slowly and cautiously at first, constantly braking with our feet. Gradually, however, we got used to it. We lifted our feet and allowed the sled to move freely for a moment and it soon sped off with great haste. We suddenly felt warm, and then, by the very first bend in the road—bam!

Our sled collided with the snowbank, throwing us off, and continued on by itself, only stopping once it had reached a second bend in the road. We tumbled several times in the snow, me on top of Sonia, then Sonia on top of me, and before we'd even had a chance to laugh it off and confirm that we were all in one piece—Another bam! Schwarzwald's sled had collided with us. He too was thrown off and all three of us rolled over each other in the snow. Sonia was the first to get up, letting out a loud and healthy laugh.

We got back up onto our sleds, and crashed a second time. But it wasn't long before we learned how to brake properly, and our journey went smoothly and enjoyably. Every now and then we had to stop and wait for Schwarzwald who was lagging behind . . .

"Hop hop!" we cried out into the night. "Schwarzwald where are you?"

"I'm here!" a voice answered us from afar—though we could not see him with our own eyes.

Sonia and I switched places; she wanted to be the driver. I held on to her waist, and soon the sled was moving at a horrendous speed. The path wound and twisted, but we were no longer being cautious and took one bend after another at great speed. We hadn't heard a sound from Schwarzwald for quite some time. Suddenly I remembered about the Devil's Grotto and brought the sled to a halt with my feet.

"We have to go on foot for this part," I said.

But, as it happened, in our haste we had already passed the Devil's Grotto. We were unaware of how fast we'd been going, and we soon arrived happily at the lower inn. We stopped to wait for Schwarzwald.

"Hop hop! hop hop!" we shouted, "Schwarzwald! Schwarzwald!"

There was no answer, just an echo which came from all sides and the stars twinkling above.

"Schwarzwald! Where are you?" I cried louder, my voice trembling. I could already sense that something had gone wrong. An inner dread gnawed at my heart.

We backtracked to search for him.

A long time passed and with each step the feeling of dread increased. We were afraid to speak, and so walked at a distance from one another. We had long since stopped shouting "Schwarzwald"; the very word had acquired a terrible meaning, and set our nerves on edge.

We walked separately, each harboring our own fear, searching in silence. Eventually we found his sled in the middle of the road.

Schwarzwald was nowhere to be found.

We began to call out his name again, shouting, searching—in vain!

"What could have happened?" Sonia asked, and her trembling voice contained a hint of anger and irritation . . .

"I fear he may have fallen in," I said.

"Fallen in?" she clutched her face in her hands and began screaming in a wild voice.

"Help! Help! Help!"

I also cried out, and all around the sound of our voices resounded so that the very mountains themselves seemed to shudder in fear.

I lit one match after another, but each time the wind blew it out, and my hands shook all the while. The idea was sheer madness at any rate: trying to see two hundred meters down into the abyss by the light of a match. I lay down on my stomach, leaning over the edge until I almost fell in myself. Sonia continued to shout.

Eventually some people arrived from above; they had heard our cries and had sled down equipped with lanterns. Everything became clear. The snowbank had been breached in one spot: that must have been where he fell in. There was nothing that could be done. There was no way to get down there in the middle of the night, and besides it would not have helped. Falling from this height, he would have died instantly.

VII

That is the story of how our friend died in the mountains. We came back down to the inn, frozen, dead-tired and shattered. We still couldn't bring ourselves to leave the place where the catastrophe had happened. It felt as though the still warm body of our poor dead friend were sitting with us, as though all we needed to do was to reach out and we could touch him. And what if? Who knows, what if he was still alive out there, calling for help?! We had stayed up there, walking back and forth, for as long as we could until we ourselves were in danger of freezing. In the end our survival instinct forced us to come down, whereupon we took a room in the hotel and spent the night. Sonia didn't get undressed. She just lay there the whole night on top of the bedsheets, her head leaning against my shoulder. I thought that she had fallen asleep like that, but without warning she began to cry and sob loudly and intensely; large tears, like drops of rain, fell from her eyes. She cried for some time, and her weeping seemed to contain as much hale vitality as her laughter, as her speech, as indeed her whole being. So it is when the happy weep, when they need to cleanse their souls of some misfortune.

Finally she drifted off on my shoulder, I laid her down onto the bed, and went outside.

The night was frosty. It was quiet all around. The white world slept, hiding within it a young life recently laid to waste.

A wild desire beckoned me toward the distant abyss. It seemed to be calling out to me, promising peace and happiness in its depths. I knew that if I went there I would never return and so I stood still, lost in my thoughts. The stars—for whom happiness and suffering, luck and misfortune, life and death are all the same—winked overhead, describing eternity.

We talked about Schwartzwald during the whole train journey back to Munich. It seemed so strange that there were only two of us instead of the three who had set off on the trip.

As we spoke, I told Sonia my theory: he hadn't fallen in as the newspapers claimed—he had jumped of his own accord.

"Do you think he really loved me?" Sonia asked. And on her face I saw that happy smile of hers.

Oh, that smile!

1908

Kol Nidre at the Music Hall

THE town of Z., which lies nestled between two mountains in a Swiss valley, was veiled in a damp fog. All day long the mountain peaks had been smouldering, choked by nebulous wisps and tendrils. But by evening the clouds had ventured down into the valley, shrouding the picturesque town, with its pointed spires, in a dull bluish haze.

A cold wind blew, creeping deep inside one's soul—A dreary, unwelcome reminder that winter could not be far off.

The famous Lake Z., which had passed the long summer content to remain within its banks reflecting streams of sunlight, seemed now to have caught cold: it trembled, uneasy ripples dashing across its surface, as though the water were repelled and panicked by the cold. Since morning the sun had been lost behind thin clouds, cheerless, without lustre, like a mourner. Now it was behind the mountains and only a few patches of crimson light remained.

Night had begun to fall.

In the streets, in the shop-windows and in the trams, lamps were being lit. A host of diffuse, blurry shafts of light pierced the fog and dispersed in all directions. A kind of sadness hovered in the twilight air: a sigh caught between day and night.

But no! The citizens of Z., strolling up and down the lakeside promenades, did not hear any sigh. These mountain folk, more accustomed to hard work than to contemplations, do not have an ear for such intangible sighs. The small, yet strong and rugged Swiss have no faculty for sadness. How beautiful and poetic their land is, how prosaic and ugly their souls must be.

But one person did hear that sigh in the depths of his heart, a foreigner, out strolling along the boulevards. He was a tall, broad-shouldered man in his forties, with a full, round face. If we take a closer look at him we notice more details: a head of black hair and a Jewish nose.

On his head he wore a top hat; on his fingers, thick golden rings (though perhaps these were merely gold-plated). No vestige of a beard or mustache was to be found on his face, a characteristic typical of his particular species: the actor.

He strolled with torpid, heedless steps, and his thoughts too were torpid and heedless.

He was a comedian at the Z. vaudeville theater, a Hungarian Jew who daily delighted the lives of the half-Jewish audience with his German rhymes and witticisms, peppered occasionally, for good measure, with homey Yiddish words.

Today the comedian was tired, sad and uncommunicative; his mind was groggy, his heart heavy.

He had been drinking the previous night and it had been late in the afternoon by the time he rose. Such awful weather! Suddenly he remembered—that very evening was Yom Kippur!

Heavy, sorrowful thoughts trudged through his mind like uninvited guests. He didn't wish to think such thoughts, but did so anyway.

Back home in Pressburg he'd left behind a wife and children—it had been a long time since he'd seen them. They wrote him letters and from time to time he would send them money. Beyond that he knew nothing of their lives . . . He glanced at his pocket watch: in half an hour he was due in the theatre.

"Blast it anyway, and this accursed fog too!"

Night had fallen. The patches of red had vanished from the sky. There was a wind blowing, and the trees trembled quietly.

"*Oh—oh—oh—kol nidre—*" he hummed under his breath, laughing internally at the melody that had suddenly come back to him. He, the humorist Didani (although his real name was Melamedzon), was beloved by his audience. Not because he had an exceptional comic talent, a sharp-wit, or a beautiful voice—in fact he was a mediocre artist as far as the profession went, perhaps even *less* than mediocre. No, he distinguished himself with the impudent way he behaved toward his audience. He talked down to them as though he were telling jokes to a small group of close friends. Nothing was off limits, anything went, whatever came into his mind, he blurted it out. The audience lapped it up, and there was a particular appetite for that authentic Jewish flavor.

"Tonight, *meine Damen und Herren*, I'm going to tell you such a *kosher* story you're simply going to *plotz* with amusement . . ." he would begin. Or if it was a Saturday evening, he would turn to the audience and say:

"In honor of Shabbes I'll tell you something nice and *Kugely* . . ." and upon hearing such familiar Yiddish words from the stage the spectators would fall into hysterics, jumping out of their skins with laughter.

"*Oy, oy, oy—veesarey,*" he continued to hum whereupon it occurred to him that it would be only right and proper if he were to mention something about Yom Kippur on stage that night. There were undoubtedly going to be plenty of Jews in the audience.

That thought, which touched upon his livelihood, helped switch his mood from the melancholy to the practical.

In the meantime he hummed Kol Nidre to himself, and the wet wind sang along with him:

". . . *ushvuey vakharamey vikhinuyey—oh—oh—oh* . . ."

Why hadn't he thought to ask the director for some time off to go to the synagogue? And what will happen after his death? What if it's all true, all that stuff about *Gehenna* and the world to come? It had completely slipped his mind that he was a Jew.

". . . *dindorno—eh—eh—eh—oh* . . ."

He had begun devising alternative lyrics to go with the melody—yes, this part went well with the words: "and this is the empty pocket."

He considered the gestures and grimaces that should accompany the song, and he could already picture how the whole theatre would resound with applause when he'd sing "and this is the empty pocket . . ." to the tune of Kol Nidre.

A fine idea, he laughed to himself.

And yet—why did he feel so sad? What was eating him up inside? A comedian shouldn't be sad; how was he supposed to perform in front of an audience in such a lousy mood?

". . . *miyom kipurim ze—eh—eh—eh* . . . !"

How *had* he ended up as a comedian anyway? How strange! he thought. After his wedding he had trained to be a ritual-slaughterer, but when he couldn't find a job he became a *badkhn*, a wedding jester. Later he somehow ended up in a second-rate music hall. If he had found a job as a *shoykhet* back home he'd be standing in the synagogue right now just like all the other Jews, wearing a *kitl* and *tallis*. He would be crying and beating his chest in repentance, and the whole place would reek of snuff.

No! A depressed comedian is no good to anyone! He struggled to drive off the melancholy thoughts, and set off in the direction of the theatre.

The twin electric lamps had already been lit and the entrance was bathed in their red glow. He went through the stage door and behind the scenes. These familiar things, the familiar preoccupations, helped him to compose himself.

The nagging in his heart subsided.

He observed the audience through an opening in the curtain and was satisfied: Jewish faces all around. There were students, every-day Jews, Russian immigrants; *those* ladies were there too, also Jewish.

"Tonight I'm going to surprise the audience," he whispered into the director's ear.

But the surprise was not a success.

He started to sing "*this is the empty pocket*" just as he had prepared, but as soon as his own ears heard the first tones of the doleful motif the nagging in his heart returned, and his voice became feeble and broken. The audience did not laugh, on the contrary: everyone seemed unhappy and they glared at him with disdain.

It seemed as if a quiet murmur were spreading through the crowd, one that sounded like the opening prayer of Yom Kippur services.

It was only through his brazen behavior that the comedian managed to get out unscathed. He stopped mid couplet, turned to the audience and said: "Help me out here will you? *oy—oy—oy* . . ."

And the audience obliged. From all sides they sang with him:

"Oy, oy, oy—veesarey . . ."

One of the ladies let out a shriek of debauched laughter, and soon the whole room was shouting:

"Bravo! Bravo! encore! . . ."

1908

Am I a Jew or a Pole?

A boarding house is like a train carriage. You arrive, someone else leaves, you have a little chat in the meantime, acquaintanceships are made that last several days, and no one takes any real interest in who you are or what you do.

It is the life of a butterfly: easy and ephemeral, leaving behind it not a trace of a lasting impression.

But little Staszek had more luck than most, by which I mean many of the other guests, having long returned to their homes, still remember him to this day. I have not forgotten him either.

A sturdy, tanned boy of about six or seven, with the dark, piercing, occasionally somewhat startled eyes typical of his race. He was invariably dressed in a light swimming costume, his bare arms and legs burned from the sun, and he was always occupied, always amused. A little inventor of new games. Out in the fresh air he was fidgety, but at the dinner table he was the calmest child you've ever seen. He sat there, eating and speaking in every respect like a grown-up, if a little more slowly. In such adult company he did not necessarily feel at home—but he was undaunted. He was a child with healthy nerves, and good sense; he could get through it.

The other guests were fond of him, always beaming. He was the first one they'd greet in the morning, and from all sides he was the recipient of warm sympathies. It was on his account, too, that one sought out the acquaintance of his parents, a young couple from Galicia.

His father was a junior lawyer, his mother a young, beautiful, brown-haired lady. A Jewish couple. Assimilated, of course.

I was the only one who recognized them as Jews, but I said nothing of it. A boarding house is no place for debates on the wretched "Jewish question." They had come here to rest after all.

But I felt sorry for the boy, a potential little convert to Christianity. Would that he could cast off that which is ugly and weak of our race! Alas, that is not how it goes.

Little Staszek conquered worlds. He accompanied his parents to climb a mountain that many adults could not manage on foot, and he returned from the difficult trek, strong and refreshed. At dinner, the owner of the boarding house gave him flowers, and the other guests did not leave him in peace for even a moment. He was the star of the boarding house—a miniature hero.

I got to know the family over the course of several days, walking together in the mountains surrounded by snow and ice. That giant, Nature, has the power to open people's hearts. Near the roar of the waterfalls, the young husband was not shy to tell me all, even about his Jewishness.

His father was a wealthy, respected man who ran a Jewish home. Two of his brothers had converted to Christianity, while the other was a Zionist. For Passover they all come together for the Seder, even the converts. They have found no solace in the bosom of their new faith. Their mother silently wipes tears from her eyes when she sees them, while their father acts as if nothing has changed, and together they celebrate Passover.

The young lady, on the other hand, had grown up in an assimilated home, raised in the Polish culture. In her father's house they dismissed the Seder with open scorn. For her, Jewishness meant *peyes* and *shtreimel* and the Sadigura Hasidim, and she hated it. An unapologetic Jewish antisemite.

I allowed myself the indiscretions of asking the young lady if Staszek, our little hero, took part in her in-laws' Passover celebrations.

It turns out that very question had caused the young couple no end of sleepless nights.

The mother does not want her son to have deep-seated impressions of a Jewish childhood, because *that*, she asserted, would cause him trouble in life. She has no desire to raise a broken Goy, like her brothers-in-law, the converts, who are uneasy when Passover comes around, feeling drawn back to the Seder and to home. She wants to raise a proper Goy, pure and simple, without complications. Let him know nothing of Passover, and later he will have no nostalgia for it. She wishes to prepare little Staszek for his life as a convert. As far as she is concerned the best thing for him would be to have him baptized without delay, but her husband is himself a broken, nostalgic Jew who runs home every Passover. What can you do with him?

In the end they did not bring Staszek with them for Passover; they left him at home with the maid.

Neither parent is satisfied: a child must have *some* sort of childhood impressions that will stay with him, some kind of religious ceremonies, a little festivity, a holiday spirit, and Staszek lacks these things. They understand this, but let's be frank: the child's mother has the more pragmatic idea.

But the young lawyer has two converts and a Zionist for brothers who do not feel remotely comfortable with the new situation, and he himself voted for a Socialist during the last elections in order to ease his Jewish conscience.

Quietly, he whispered in my ear, "Assimilation has gone bankrupt."

That is to say, *he himself* has gone bankrupt, but that is something he did not seem to recognize.

Incidentally, he's a busy man. He does not have a high opinion of the political speechmakers, neither the Zionists nor the assimilationists. There is too much corruption in Galicia; the Poles are antisemites, so he voted for a Socialist, though by nature he is afraid of the Socialists.

That's how little Staszek is growing up, a fresh, sturdy sapling unaware that over his innocent head hovers the Jewish Question with all its gravity.

And perhaps he does know? Children think much more seriously than we give them credit for. They do not listen when we chatter, when we are not speaking from the heart. But to an earnest discussion they prick up their ears, and their eyes twinkle with curiosity.

One time, as we were walking together uphill, we spoke about Jews. Staszek usually overtook us with his little legs. But this time he walked alongside us, and it did not occur to us that he was listening to our conversation. Suddenly he drew close to his father, took him by the hand, and blurted out a question:

"*Powiedz mnie, Tatusiu, ja jestem Polak czy 'Żyd*'?" ("Tell me, father, am I a Pole or a Jew?")

"What a question!" The young man glanced at his wife, while I watched them both. Staszek however demanded an answer; he wanted to know. It was a question concerning his life and he did not know the answer.

"*Niech mi tatuś powie.*" ("Tell me, father.")

His father found himself in an awkward position. It's quite possible that, had I not been there, he would have simply answered, "a Pole," but for my benefit he responded, "*Ty jesteś Żyd-Polak.*" ("You're a Jew-Pole.")

Staszek, however, did not understand the answer. It was as though he had been told: "cold-hot" or "black-white". . . He knew there were two categories of people: a respectable, noble group and a second, disrespectable, lowly group to which it was shameful to belong. He had been raised with such notions, and his real question had been: am I unfortunate, or fortunate? Will things go well or badly for me? You're unfortunate-fortunate, things are good-bad, you are a Jew-Pole . . . a child's mind is not yet corrupted enough to understand such things.

He protested, demanded an answer.

"Tell me the truth, father..."

His mother answered in a harsh, angry tone:

"*Ty jesteś Polak.*" ("You are a Pole.") Staszek's questions stopped. He followed us silently, lost in his thoughts.

But he was not satisfied.

That night, just as we had returned from our mountain trek, and were strolling outside, I noticed Staszek walking very close beside me; he wanted to catch me alone. I walked away to the side, and Staszek was soon beside me again. He asked me quietly, in confidence:

"*Niech mi pan powie naprawdę, ja jestem Żyd czy Polak?*" ("Tell me honestly: am I a Jew or a Pole?")

Poor child! I didn't have the heart to tell him the truth, that his parents had lied to him. I lifted him up in my arms and kissed his forehead.

"*Niech mi pan powie . . .*" he asked again.

"You're a good, clever child," I told him, "and when you're old enough, you'll see for yourself . . ."

And he left me, angry and unsatisfied. His last opportunity of getting a straight answer had failed him.

He did not play games that evening.

The Jewish Question accompanied him to his bed.

1911

Ishmael is our Uncle

THE owner of the boarding house announced the happy news that we had new company; "Russians" had arrived—two ladies from Moscow.

Whenever you're abroad and you hear the word "Russians," you think to yourself: our own kind, brothers, Sons of Israel, naturally.

What more do you need? I myself, a Jewish sinner from Warsaw count as a "Russian" when I'm abroad. A fine Russian I make!

At dinner I observed the new guests. Definitely Jewish: Jewish eyes, Jewish noses and—Jewish foreignness.

What do I mean by "Jewish foreignness"? It's hard to say. But you recognize it the same way you recognize a gatecrasher at a wedding. Our brothers, the Sons of Israel are easy to spot.

We soon made each other's acquaintance. I don't recall how the topic came up, but one of the ladies said to me, in Russian of course: "Actually we are Germans, Russified Lutherans."

You should always take people by their word. True, I had heard them speaking German; very *daytshmerish* with great fanfare, a mutilated, broken language. But what do I know, maybe they had already forgotten their mother tongue. Moscow is the heart of Russia after all, and has a strong Russifying influence.

Afterwards the younger of the two told me that she had once been to Vilna, that Vilna is a very fine city, but—"there are an awful lot of Jews there."

"An awful lot of Jews"—So, I was dealing with a Russified German with a Jewish face, and an antisemite to boot. I respond: "Certainly, Vilna is a Jewish city, I myself am a Jew and have lived there."

My answer made no impression on her.

I'm a Jew and suddenly she's no longer an antisemite; our acquaintanceship is entirely unaffected by the whole thing.

Then I discovered that she was a student, and that she was known to work eighteen hour shifts in order to afford a ticket to a Stanislavski performance.

Something suspiciously Jewish about that too.

Suddenly—a development. Someone had come to join the ladies: a Turk, a genuine Turk with a red hat, who had brought real Turkish tobacco with him from Constantinople.

I happen to be something of an expert when it comes to Turkish tobacco. You can't pull the wool over my eyes in that department.

He was a Turk, and what's more, a Young Turk, and we soon began discussing politics, speaking about the Albanian uprising and even about Zionism.

"There's no antisemitism where I come from. The Jews and the Turks are brotherly peoples," he told me.

Fine, but it was all getting a bit much. A strange puzzle of post-Babel proportions: Germans from Moscow who don't know any German, an antisemitic student, a Lutheran, Jewish faces, and by their side—by all accounts the suitor of one of the ladies—a Turk.

It wasn't until a week later, when the enigma had grown even more complex, that it began to unravel.

The girls' father arrived, a raw face and a Jewish face. I could have sworn that he was a former Nikolayevsky soldier.

I was not mistaken. I happened to walk past the old man's door and heard his voice. Yiddish, the Yiddish of a Nikolayevsky soldier.

"I want to live as a Jew here, *panimayete*? Go yourselves and leave me be, I'm not traveling anywhere on Shabbes.

Modern Marranos, I was beginning to understand. But where does the Turk fit into the story?

I did not rest idle, and when I encountered the old man out for a walk by himself, I approached him, offered him my hand in the Jewish manner and simply came out with it:

"*Sholem aleykhem, aleykhem Sholem*, are you also a Jew?"

We spoke about the weather, as is appropriate, and about the persecution of Jews. And as we got to know each other a little better, I discovered the secret. The old man told me everything.

His daughters were Muslims. They'd *wanted* to become Germans, wanted to take on the Lutheran faith, but the old man had not allowed it, and they'd had no choice but to follow his wishes. The daughters could not seem to accept what had come to pass against their wills, and so they continued to identify as Germans

"I told them, those 'Germans' of mine, that if they converted to Christianity or married a Christian man, I would no longer be their father. *Pashli von!* No dowry and no inheritance.

Go ahead. I don't want to know you anymore, you want to live in Moscow? Fine. Convert to Islam. How does the saying go, *nye pravda li*, Ishmael is our uncle after all."

And he sighed, slowly shaking his head.

It is dire. Those Christians, they hate the Jews—Lutherans, Catholics, Orthodox, they're all the same. With Muslims on the other hand it's an entirely different story. My eldest has a Turkish fiancé—a *poriadotshni molodoy tshelovyek*. What can you say? What can you do? It's not what I wanted, God is my witness. But convert to Christianity—not that either. The Muslims are the Ishmaelites after all. What do you say? Is that any better? I pounded the table and said: '*khristianskaya* faith—*nye razershayu.*[1] And they obeyed me, *nye posmieli* . . ."

I regarded the old man. He lived like one at war with the whole world and its many faiths, holding a grudge for the myriad injustices suffered by the Jews.

---

1 The Christian faith—I will not allow it!

"Ishmael is our uncle." And yet when the family was together, the old man held himself constantly aloof from his future son-in-law. I can't say I ever saw him speak a word in his direction. He was clearly not overjoyed to someday become grandfather to little Ishmaelites in little red hats.

Ishmael is an uncle: *Only* an uncle mind you—not quite immediate family.

1911

By a Lonely Grave

I met him in the mountains on my way to an alpine village that lies buried in a narrow pass on the edge of a fast stream. I wanted to spend the night there before moving on higher the next morning. He, on the other hand, had no intention of going any further.

I soon realised that he was not your typical tourist. He knew the village well, telling me that it was home to both Catholics and Protestants, that there were two churches and two graveyards and that he knew some people there.

He came from the far north, from Norway, and was not overly fond of Switzerland.

"You should really see Norway some day," he told me. "The fjords, the bright nights, the cliffs! You must promise to visit me there next summer, to see for yourself."

I couldn't figure out what kind of man he was, what he was doing there, or why, catching up with me on his long legs, he plunged so eagerly into conversation that he was already inviting me to visit him in Norway. What was in it for him?

"You're a Russian aren't you?" he asked.

"Yes, certainly, a Jew from Russia," I said

"Of course that's what I meant. Exactly! Exactly!"

He'd had an acquaintance once; she too had been a Jew from Russia . . . And I began to understand the intimacy that had developed so quickly between us. Incidentally, the man made quite a strong, unsettling impression; he was tall and blond, built like a giant, but with soft, strangely child-like, blue eyes. He spoke naïvely, but his movements were energetic. He was one of those people whose simple words contain the echo of long and deep torment and yearning, which undermine even their best attempts at smiling, and linger on in our memories of them.

We arrived just as darkness was falling; the surrounding snowy peaks still shimmered faintly in a pinkish glow. I was tired, and prepared myself for a sleepless, nerve-ridden night.

Oh, I know those moonlit nights in the mountains! As the air cools at night, the sky wraps itself up in a gray fog and it seems as though a storm is coming. But then, the slightest wind is enough to drive the fog away and the moon breaks through, pouring out an intoxicating brightness. If you look out the window, you'll see the snow gleaming in the moonlight. From far and near you can hear the music of the Alps ringing out: the bells of livestock grazing in the white night on the pastures, wandering around, far from human eyes, with their shadows—uphill, downhill, ringing, ringing. The stream and waterfalls murmur ceaselessly. Nature lives its life and sings its abundant song. Such nights are not made for sleeping. On nights like those, if you happen to carry some vague hope in your heart, or if you have perhaps someone close to you, a dear friend, a lover, then you'll end up thinking about them into the wee small hours, until the first rays of sunlight appear. Only corpses, or young, withered souls, can rest there and sleep. I know those moonlit nights in the mountains.

I lay there like a prisoner, in my room filled with moonlight, for a long time, my eyes open, breathing in the sharp, cool mountain air, which intoxicates just like the brightness, just like the far-off bells, ringing from the valley below. I got out of bed. It was already well past midnight. I went over to the window and saw the long shadow of a man. I looked carefully and recognized the outline of my new acquaintance, the Norwegian, striding off into the white night, apparently without aim, lost in his own thoughts, distracted.

"If I'm not disturbing you," I called out to him, "I'll get dressed and come down. Who can sleep during a night like this?"

"Good," he answered curtly, a moment later shouting back to me, "but I'd advise you to bring your cape and a scarf. There's a cold wind blowing from the mountains."

I did as he advised and was soon standing next to him. He was silent now; his demeanor had grown less childish and more serious. I thought to myself that this man was not out of place on a night like this; he had some connection to it. You could almost hear something buzzing in his heart without let-up. Like a mountain stream, there was something alive within him, singing in him, and he couldn't control it, couldn't get over it. It wouldn't let him free.

He had been in love with a Jewish girl, a dead girl, who lay buried here in this village, in her own separate corner of the Protestant graveyard. He confided his sad tale to me, telling it with all the naïvety and trust of a child. He was sure that the tragic destiny of that girl would be a subject as close to my heart as it was to his. Like all Gentiles he had a strong belief in the solidarity and brotherhood of all Jews. His lover, in a way, was connected to me, almost like family, almost like a sister.

It had happened about six years before; he'd been studying in Zurich and fell in love with the Jewish girl. What sort of a woman was she that she could capture and dominate a stranger from the distant north? He described her: pale, with brown hair and large, black eyes; she was quiet and attentive, with an unusual, melodic voice.

She was exactly—so he told me—like a locked harp: taut, shivering strings which hummed silently to themselves. She wasn't everyone's type—she was no great beauty—she was only for him that had the key, who could touch the strings. But what a temperament, what inner life revealed itself then! She was normally silent, contemplative, prone to melancholy—but how lively she could be when it was just you and her; how she could talk and talk without end, chirping like a little bird. There are types of people which nature only creates once, just one single copy, and she was one of those.

And she loved him and gave herself over to him with all the energy of her hidden temperament. They decided to get married, but for that she needed to convert.

"It's remarkable," he told me, "how attached you people are to that religion of yours. She wasn't in the least observant, but even I know what torment it was for her until she finally relented. Long, long nights without sleep, long days going around like mad, until love, her first love, finally overcame her and convinced her to take that step."

The only obstacle was her parents. They were well off, cultivated people. She hoped to get their blessing, traveling all the way home with that express purpose, but once she got there, she found herself unable to say a single word to them about it. The anti-Jewish pogroms were in full swing in Russia at that time, and her parents had suffered because of them. She returned, tired and broken, not knowing what to do. In the end she confided her secret to her brother who was studying in Bern. He telegraphed their parents and her father came out immediately. She had to give him her word that she wouldn't convert. Once her father left, mollified, I came to her room and barely recognized her; she was terribly distraught, pale and sad.

"What is it, my love?"

She didn't tell me the whole story but I could tell that something was amiss.

"You don't love me anymore?"

"Oh, don't talk! Don't talk! Please . . ."

"But her voice, her kisses and her eyes told me more about her love than could ever be expressed in words, and we set off together into the mountains, here to this very village. In this very hotel she poisoned herself after one long, hot night of love.

She wrote me a letter telling the story of what happened with her brother and father. In a separate letter to her parents, whom she loved deep down, she said her goodbyes and asked that her body should not be disturbed. She wanted to be buried here."

And so went the sad tale of a Jewish girl who lies buried in an Alpine village, in her own private corner of the Protestant graveyard.

We continued walking in the moonlit night until we came to the little cemetery that surrounded the church. Low gravestones and crosses twinkled in the light. On the gravestones, one could read short inscriptions from the living to the dead, in the modest style of country folk. We continued until we reached a certain corner with a small iron fence surrounding a flat stone. The Norwegian, unselfconscious despite my presence, knelt down in his childlike naïvety. Leaning against the fence, he knelt in silence. Mute.

And all the while, the far-off bells continued to ring and the waterfalls murmured without cease.

1911

Shiringer's Demise

I

WHEN Shiringer strolls through the streets of Berlin he is accompanied by a collection of beautiful things. Every item about his person—from the hat on his head all the way down to the polished shoes on his feet, sparkling and dandyish—seems to announce to the world: "look how beautiful we are!"

And Shiringer, a broad-shouldered, thirty-five year old of medium height, was himself one of those beautiful things. Clean-shaven, well fed, and with a wicked fire in his dark searching eyes he stood out from the gray bustling masses. He also distinguished himself from the other pedestrians by his leisurely pace. He moved with a regularity and reserve that had come under strict doctor's orders: plenty of walks, but no hurrying under any circumstances!

The streets parted for him; it wasn't uncommon for someone to step out of his path with the instinctive certainly that it must be so. Women, and girls on the cusp of adulthood in particular, twisted around to shower him with glances, like clouds of pollen. Some smiled at him, but they seldom received a smile in return. Shiringer had no confidence in his own facial muscles. A troubled childhood and early youth had schooled him to be cautious. Besides, there was no smile that went well with his severe, unmoving face. Whenever he did attempt to smile it would come out as such a frightful grimace that the effect was alienating and repulsive.

No sooner had he entered the café than his searching eyes had taken the measure of every corner. He unraveled the silk scarf from around his neck, removed his leather gloves, put away his light overcoat and hat, and pulled his trousers up a little before sitting down: but there were plenty of beautiful items left, a tie, a diamond pin, the ring on his finger, a golden chain, etc. etc.

He had a habit of clearing his throat before speaking, to buy a little time. The waiter who had come to take his order was left standing there for a moment while Shiringer finished his little cough, only after which he was ready to order a seltzer-water. The café was mostly empty except for the regulars who almost never left the place: women of dubious repute, failed artists and morphine addicts.

As it happened Shiringer had not entered the café willingly. He was having a financial dispute with a certain Mr. Sekol involving a matter of currency-speculation and seeing that same Mr. Sekol coming down the street—not having enough time to turn around and escape—Shiringer had ducked into the café to avoid him.

But once inside, his gaze came to rest upon a figure with a long, thin face and pointed chin sitting at one of the tables. He tried to tear his eyes away, but they were drawn to that face. He was flustered: Shiringer was a nervous man, ever since the war when he had been captured by the Germans and hospitalized for shellshock. Later he had done hard labor in a prison camp until he pulled off a daring escape. It was only after the war that he became absurdly wealthy.

The long-faced figure turned to Shiringer and bored into him with gray, piercing eyes. The stranger soon stood up, unfolding to his full height. He was tall and thin-boned, and dressed in a French military jacket that was just a little too short for him, making him appear taller still. The stranger approached Shiringer, arms outstretched, and they embraced.

Shiringer felt overwhelmed. If it were up to him he would prefer not to kiss such a fearsome and unsettling face. Gradually he recognized who it was: it was Vasilyev, the sergeant of his regiment during those wild, terrible events in the Polish village when, during one twenty-four hour period, the village had passed four times from the hands of one army to the other, under the constant thrusting of bayonets.

Vasilyev took a seat next to him and spoke openly, in the Russian manner, about everything he had been through. He had survived the war and the revolution, had fought in Denikin's volunteer army during the civil war that followed, then under General Wrangel's command he had attained the rank of colonel before eventually finding himself here in Berlin in search of work.

An unfamiliar shudder passed through Shiringer's body—Denikin's army, he thought: Vasilyev probably had a hand in the pogroms!

Shiringer would have liked to heap insults on him, to stand up and flee. But Vasilyev was fixing him in such a strange manner. In the chaos of his memories of those wild events, the image of Vasilyev swam into focus, commanding:

"Bayonets, at the ready!" he'd roared, springing toward Shiringer, looking directly at him, scrutinizing him with such a devilish gaze, as though accusing him of wanting to run away and hide somewhere.

And Shiringer recalled how a group of Germans emerged suddenly from behind a wall. He saw them charge right toward them, enraged, eyes glazed over, rifles extended. His knees buckled and he fell to the ground. Then Vasilyev slapped him across the back of his neck, "Get up!" Then he stood up, grabbed his rifle and charged, plunging his bayonet through an enemy soldier's face. Blood gushed from the eye socket and the enemy fell. Vasilyev rammed the butt of his rifle into the fallen man's head, and gray matter squirted out.

Vasilyev was coming to the end of a long speech, after which he asked Shiringer for a loan. Only then, when things turned to money-matters, did Shiringer regain his composure and find the strength to think clearly.

"But you're a *pogromchik*, you've murdered Jews!"

Vasilyev swore, making the sign of the cross, that he had never harmed a single Jew. And though Shiringer did not believe him—for Vasilyev had momentarily lost his childlike openness and his gray eyes could no longer return Shiringer's gaze—he nevertheless handed over several marks to be rid of him.

This brief encounter left Shiringer terribly shaken, and it took him several hours to recover. Fragmentary recollections from that strange time flooded his mind and he lost all sense of time passing; he did not know when it was night or when day, when it began or when it ended. The images—a surge, an explosion, blood, falling and getting back up—nothing was clear, like outlines from a half-forgotten dream. But in the background of all those memories stood the figure of Vasilyev, and Shiringer's heavy panting, which he seemed to hear even now.

II

Shiringer emerged from the café in a state of agitation. It was past one in the afternoon on a late summer's day. It was still warm enough to enjoy lunch outdoors in the fresh air. Back when Shiringer had been a factory-clerk in Warsaw, during those long years of labor, he had always observed his manager who lived well and enjoyed the finer things in life. Shiringer now imitated him in all things. But he felt anxious. It was as though his brain had been shaken up and everything that had been buried at the bottom came up to the surface; his thoughts were now muddy. The color had drained from his face, and even his elegant accessories seemed to have lost their lustre.

He did not go to the stock exchange that day, and had missed lunch. It was five in the evening by the time he came around. He had arranged a rendezvous with one of his lady-friends. He brought her to an expensive restaurant, ordered wine, and afterwards they drove in an automobile. The lady was impressed by his generosity and taste for indulgence. She clung to him, relishing his jubilant mood and the uncharacteristic affection he showed her. He seemed to her like an entirely new person. She was a middle class girl whose parents had suffered greatly during the war. She'd found a job in an office, gradually growing accustomed to the lifestyle of an office girl, and found herself a "sweetheart." Yet she had a sentimental streak: deep down she was still a girl waiting to find a husband. She had feelings for Shiringer; she was impressed by the brutal energy he sometimes displayed before her. Today he'd been gentle. But why was the crease in his hat not in the right place? And why was there a sadness in his eyes? She also sensed something of his unease, and nestled up to him all the closer.

"What a funny day today," she said.

"There's nothing funny about it, Mitsy. It's high time I got married. Life is dreary when one is alone."

But a moment later he had changed his mind and added:

"It's not you I want to marry of course. You're good as a lover, not as a wife."

She fell silent, a hangdog expression on her face. Shiringer amused himself by pestering her with questions.

"You're not angry with me, are you, Mitsy? What ever for?"

"I didn't say anything."

He put his arm around her and hugged her tightly, which made them both feel less awkward. He looked her up and down, appraising her with the eyes of a businessman inspecting his merchandise. His unspoken verdict: A fine woman, still attractive, though not as young as she used to be.

But as his eyes lingered over his female companion, something incomprehensible happened to Shiringer. With terrible clarity a memory flashed before his eyes—from that half-forgotten day. It was as if it were right there in front of him: *there* was the shadow of the house, and *there* was the white, cascading light of the village. A short distance away, the roar of a machine gun chanting its deathly refrain. Shvartsberg crashes into him with his shoulder, he falls. But as he falls he grabs onto Shiringer's leg with both hands, and lies there, dead. Shiringer felt, or he imagined he felt, the hands of that dead soldier clutching at his leg. At first he stood rooted to the spot and though that this was it, surely his end had come—he could no longer move, could no longer defend himself. He lay like that, stretched out on the ground for some time until an alarm was sounded and once again soldiers where charging head on with outstretched rifles. He did not remember how he had freed his leg from the dead man's clutches.

He ordered the chauffeur to stop the car and bid a cold farewell to Mitsy whose eyes were full of tears.

"What are you crying about now?" He asked angrily, "I'm not in the mood today—can't you see that?'

"I wasn't crying," the young woman answered defensively.

In his thoughts Shiringer was venting his anger toward Mr. Sekol, the speculator on account of whom he had gone into that café in the first place. He cursed him with the harshest words. He was afraid to even think about Vasilyev. It was clear that some misfortune was hovering over Shiringer. Impossible to escape. He suddenly felt a burning hatred toward all things. On his finger shone a diamond ring, and Shiringer hated even that.

I have no one on my side, he thought. Everyone is against me. And why? Because I was lucky, because I pulled myself up out of poverty. Even my own brother hits me up for money, as if he has it coming, and he thinks in his heart: "Rich on the spoils of war!" Even Mitsy reproaches me for not buying her silk stockings . . .

He was seething inside. He stormed down the street toward his house and completely forgot that his doctor had forbidden him from walking too quickly.

That night, as he undressed, he remembered the spot on his leg where the dead man's hands had dug in.

Shiringer never recovered from that shock. It was just not to be. The former clerk who had so cunningly and tirelessly pulled himself up out of hardship was not destined to enjoy the pleasures of this world. He abandoned all of his elegant accessories, and began to maunder like a lost shadow.

He was haunted by a terrible dream. Regularly, almost twice a week it came to him: Shvartsberg dragging him by the leg, down into the grave, pulling and tugging until Shringer awoke, soaked in sweat.

He traveled to the mountains; the dream followed. He went back home, to Warsaw, to visit relatives; the dream pursued him there too . . .

Until one morning, having returned to Berlin, he noticed red marks—what looked like finger marks—on his right leg, on the same spot where Shvartsberg had held him.

It took all his energy to stifle the screams.

He hastened to the doctor, and the doctor had him sent to the hospital so that the professors there should see this strange case for themselves

And there in that hospital Shiringer met his demise.

1923

The Rebbe's Grandson

I

THE terrace of the large café in Berlin was almost empty; only a few tables here and there were occupied. It was almost autumn and the weather was becoming unpredictable: there was already a strange, newly arrived chill in the air. At one table, surrounded by empty chairs, tables and a general atmosphere of neglect, sat a man who one would guess to be about forty years of age. Berelzon, Doctor of Philosophy, was his name. He did not like to sit amid a crowd of strangers; he always felt lost in a packed coffee house. Besides, the weather that day had energized him; his imagination was alive, freeing him from the apathy and weariness that had weighed him down of late. As he ran his hand over his brow, and slowly rubbed his eyes, his mind was filled with memories, scattered and blurred like the thin clouds that raced overhead across the gloomy sky: memories of the trilled call of the shofar, of the wail of supplications, of the Rebbe's white satin, and of heavy hearts voicing their lamentations to the heavens.

He was accompanied by his wife, who sat all but invisible next to him. Berelzon was one of those people who stand out, hard to ignore: a full-blooded Jewish type, with a thick black beard, and a long finely-chiseled nose.

From his grandfather and great-grandfather he had inherited his stately, rabbinical appearance, and his dark eyes contained a hint of that strange sadness of a privileged only child. His wife in contrast was slight, with a somewhat sickly countenance. The only thing one could read—after lengthy consideration—from her face was a strong, typically feminine stubbornness, which had left its mark around the corners of her small mouth and thin, bleached lips.

Thoughts pulsed feverishly through the bearded man's mind. In such moments everything around him seemed to take on extra meaning and importance: people's faces seemed more expressive, even the clothes they wore and how they moved seemed to have something to tell him; laden with import were the little birds that hopped on the street, pecking for food between the cobblestones; and the golden cross on the large church opposite seemed to shake as though it too were a living member of the animal kingdom. The buildings cast shadows that seemed to spread unease as they crept across the street, appearing and reappearing in unison with the clouds overhead. Everything became livelier, breathing the air of eternity, and he, the living man with his watchful eye and mind, felt closer to the world—a mere step away from uncovering its ultimate secret, its hidden ways.

Why was it not our fate to be like the clouds, which come and go, collecting the earth's dust, taking on different forms, disappearing again, becoming nothing, all in order to be born anew?

Berelzon mumbled these words to himself, though he knew his little wife was eavesdropping on his soliloquy; he could sense her strained attention though he did not look in her direction. His words—he realized—were not falling into the void; they were being intercepted, recorded, by a logical mind that he loved well.

Because the little wife was, in his isolation, his only admirer. He had her to thank that he could rise above his own worthlessness. What did he, Dr. Berelzon, represent for all the others besides a beard and a nice suit?

As he pondered and spoke he kept one hand—the one on which he wore his wedding ring—on the table. A strong respectable hand, somewhat hairy. The sharp bright eyes of his little wife fixed on that hand; she could not look away. Her contemplation was strained by the desire to reach out and touch his hand, for she loved her husband with the passion of a young woman. With each passing day her love grew just as her youth faded. She felt as though she were blushing when her soft hand caressed his, feeling the coarse touch of his skin.

His hand twitched under hers; his gaze, which had been lost in the indistinct void, met hers with a flash of estrangement. It lasted only a split second. She sighed and took back her hand. She did not have a mirror and so could only consider a small portion of her outward appearance: the contours of her declining breasts. But that was enough for her. With a cold prudence she began to suspect that a shift had occurred in their erotic balance. She once again looked at him with a mixture of exaltation and regret: he was still a thriving man in his best years!

And as if to spite her, on all sides young female figures roved—svelte, limber bodies, each with her own promise. They came accompanied by men, or they passed flirtatiously alone and not one of them failed to feast her eyes on Berelzon. The small woman was crestfallen. She pressed her lips tighter and her eyes stared with renewed stubbornness, sparkling like green polished steel.

II

But there was another reason for Dr. Berelzon's withdrawal into himself. That very day he had received a letter from Reb Yisokher-Ber, a landholder in Eastern Galicia who'd been his secret ally and benefactor ever since Berelzon had left the house of his grandfather the Rebbe (his father died young and so he was raised in his grandfather's house). The letter had shaken him, not so much for its contents but for the clear signs of old-age and impermanency which were so noticeable in the handwriting. The once shapely, angular letters, embellished with fine, elegant ornamentation, were now scrawled by a trembling hand. Sometimes a letter, and in places a whole word, was missing. People like Reb Yisokher-Ber, powerful, influential people, reach a certain level of infirmity beyond which they cannot function, and their days are numbered: that is what the handwriting told him. And then there was the tone of the letter itself.

It was written in old Hebrew, but noteworthy was the absence of the traditional expression *Bezres hashem*, with God's help. Yisokher-Ber wrote about his condition in the wake of the terrible experiences of recent times. Some of his children had died during the war, others had emigrated far and wide, only one daughter still lived with him, the half-crazy one. His wealth had also taken a hit and he was just about hanging on to his land. "And I feel as though my strength is waning and I am just waiting for you, the light of my eyes, to come and illuminate the darkness. And when will your book come out, the one I've long been waiting so impatiently to read?

A life was being snuffed out, wasting away without a hint of solace, Dr. Berelzon thought, going over the last words of the letter in his mind. He felt somehow disturbed, somehow guilty about the infirmity of his old friend. Why does *this* of all letters, perhaps the last he will ever read from his friend, lack—as though on purpose—the traditional mention of God's name.

Because Reb Yisokher-Ber never allowed thoughts which could destroy his life. He believed in the Rebbe and had also believed in the Rebbe's grandson, the apostate. He believed he would bring a great light to the world. It was not for nothing that the professors in Bern had been so impressed by the boy, that they had honored him profusely. You could rely on young Elimeylekh Berelzon, he always thought. He supported him throughout his studies with money, and he knew he was preparing an important volume that was set to revolutionize philosophy. Berelzon felt a sense of panic in the letter, a fear of leaving the world without seeing the day when Elimeylekh's name would ring out all over the world and people of all faiths, Jews and Gentiles alike, would see a great light.

These last years Dr. Berelzon felt like he'd been biding time. The war, which had passed like a bad dream taking his best years, had not been a period of productivity or inspiration. But the war was over; now there was no question of putting aside the work. He prepared himself and waited for a wind to fill his sails, spurring him to finish his life's work *Man and the Cosmos.*

Dr. Berelzon was buried in thought; he remembered the tall, strong, pot-bellied Reb Yisokher-Ber as he'd seen him twenty years previously when last Berelzon had been a guest on his estate. They had walked uphill in the Carpathian landscape toward the waterfall, which bubbled down into the chasm below. There was a joy and a fondness that radiated from the man who had always consoled Berelzon, and with a wave of his large, strong hands he gave him to understand that things would be ok, there was no cause for concern, that God would see him through.

"As long as you are earnest," he'd said, shouting to be heard over the roar of the cascading water. "No one needs to tell me what you're capable of, Elimeylekh. I know who you are. There's not many like you, and with such a noble line of ancestors watching over you! . . ."

Berelzon had been standing still, staring down into the chasm, and as he looked up he met Reb Yisokher-Ber's eyes regarding him with such affection and delight.

"Do you really want to go abroad? God forbid, but there'll be heartache . . ."

"It is unavoidable—It must be so," Berelzon had replied sharply.

Yisokher-Ber was still standing over him, in his yellow boots, looking at him with eyes that demanded something in return:

"I'm a simple man," he said shamefully with a helpless smile, his large frame beginning to sway as it did when studying the holy texts, "how can I comprehend such things? I'd like you to explain . . ."

Yisokher-Ber had an urge to hear his thoughts; he could not stand those arid words: "it must be so."

And within Berelzon began to stir the instincts of his grandfathers and great-grandfathers, which taught him how to deal with thirsty human souls. He spoke with the solemnity of the Torah at the Rebbe's table.

"The water falls into the chasm, whether it wants to or not, and the streams become rivers and all the rivers run into the sea; yet the sea is not full . . .

". . . *vehayam eynoynu mole* . . . unto the place from whence the rivers come, thither they return again," Yisokher-Ber mumbled, shaking his head earnestly.

After that Yisokher-Ber took Berelzon home and they drank a glass of strong brandy. Some Hasidim arrived, but Yisokher-Ber did not permit anyone to disturb Berelzon.

Everything had been arranged: a secret pact between the two men, which the Hasidim had no business interfering with . . .

Yisokher-Ber was moved by the thought that he, and he alone, stood by Elimeylekh's side . . .

And this very friend had now begun to slip into the shadows. The world was becoming hollower, eaten through by worms, unless a new great light should come to fill the gaps.

Two ladies entered the café and occupied the table next to theirs. They stole glances at Berelzon. One even smiled at him as bold as brass. Berelzon once again felt the rush of blood in his veins that had so often assaulted him of late.

And his little wife entreated:

"Let's go home . . . It's getting late."

1926/1927

Translator's Postface

AT the turn of the twentieth century, Yiddish, as the vernacular language of the overwhelming majority of Ashkenazi Jewry, was widely spoken throughout the Russian and Austro-Hungarian empires as well as Romania and in significant immigrant communities in numerous cities throughout Western Europe and the Americas. Nevertheless, the act of writing in Yiddish was never a self-evident or neutral one. While European literature had long been dominated by linguistic giants such as French, English, German, and Russian, the eighteenth and nineteenth centuries saw a growing awakening of national consciousness throughout the continent, with smaller national languages agitating for recognition and prestige. The Jews of Eastern Europe found themselves at a crossroads: should they write in Hebrew, a liturgical tongue that formed (along with Aramaic) the basis for traditional Jewish literacy? Or should they write in Yiddish, a language largely dismissed as a *zhargon* (jargon), but which had nevertheless served as the principal idiom of Ashkenazic Jewry since the eleventh century?

For the Maskilim, proponents of the Haskalah (Yid: *haskole*) or so-called Jewish Enlightenment, the revival of Hebrew as a modern literary language was one of the pillars of their movement. Their other objective was the propagation of secular ideas and modern pedagogy in Jewish communities, where they perceived widespread religious dogma and superstition. However, in order to reach a wider audience for their ideology, the Maskilim found themselves obliged to also produce material in the vernacular language of the Jewish masses: Yiddish.

What began as a means to an end soon evolved into an end in its own right and so, by the end of the nineteenth century, authors such as Isaac Meyer Dik (1807–1893) and Mendele Moykher Sforim (1836–1917) had succeeded in transforming Yiddish into a medium for literary expression, and they in turn inspired writers such as Sholem Aleichem (1859–1916) and Isaac Leybush Peretz (1852–1915) who would lay the foundations for modern Yiddish literature as we know it.

Hersh Dovid Nomberg was born in 1876 in Mszczonów (known as Ashminov in Yiddish) a market town about thirty miles from Warsaw, then part of the Russian Empire. He grew up in a strictly religious Hasidic environment. His father died young and he was raised mostly by his maternal grandfather. As a child, Nomberg contracted tuberculosis and was sent to recover in a sanatorium in Otwock, fourteen miles south of Warsaw. He survived, but would suffer from chronic health problems for much of his life. He showed promise as a scholar and was sent to yeshiva in Radomsk, where he excelled, gaining a reputation as a Talmudic prodigy. At eighteen he married Masha Shpiro, the eldest daughter of a wealthy local merchant, before he had even finished his yeshiva education. This was followed by three years of room and board courtesy of his new in-laws. By now he had two sons, Moyshe and Eliezer. Masha's father rented them a house and premises in town and they set up a food shop. Nomberg didn't take to this new lifestyle. By all accounts a terrible shopkeeper, soon Nomberg's store became a notorious venue for idling and card playing.

At around this time he abandoned his religious studies and began experimenting with forbidden literature. He started with Maskilic texts—secular writing in modern Hebrew—which acted as a gateway drug leading on to Hebrew poetry, and eventually literature in non-Jewish languages—Russian, German—exposing him to new ideas and writers: Western philosophy, Spinoza, Dostoyevsky, Schopenhauer etc. . . . When his father-in-law discovered what was happening he was enraged and closed down the shop for good.[1]

Nomberg set off for Warsaw to find work. His first port of call was Isaac Leybush Peretz, the most famous Yiddish writer of the time, whose poetry had left a deep impression on Nomberg. Peretz praised Nomberg's poems and advised him to try his hand at writing in Yiddish. Nomberg returned to Radomsk and began to write poems and stories in Hebrew, which were soon being published in newspapers. Disagreements with his father-in-law eventually came to a head and he was forced to grant a divorce and leave behind his three sons (he would, however, keep in contact

---

1 "Der ile fun radomsk", *Sefer yizkor lekehilat radomsk*, (Tel-Aviv, 1967), 274–275.

with them). And so at the age of twenty-one he returned to Warsaw with the ambition of earning a living as a writer.

Nomberg became a contributor to various newspapers as translator, journalist, editor, and columnist in both Yiddish and Hebrew. At the same time he earned early acclaim for his short prose pieces which were praised for their psychological insight. To quote Nomberg's German translator, Abraham Sühl:

> "When [Nomberg] describes the landscape and its atmosphere, as in his story 'In the Mountains,' for example, he does so not in the style of a lyrical poet, developing his own impressions and weaving them into a motif for its own sake, rather he depicts them with an eye to how they are perceived by his characters. His angle is psychological motivation."[1]

1 Abraham Suhl, preface to *Flügelmann: Novellen aus dem Jüdischen* (Leipzig: Schemesch Verlag, 1924), iv.

Several of Nomberg's stories from this period were published in competing Hebrew and Yiddish versions, often adapted and self-translated in such a way that it is difficult to say which version was the original.[1] With the closure of the Yiddish daily newspaper, *Der Veg*, in 1907, he left Warsaw to travel around Western Europe, spending time in France, Germany and Switzerland. The bulk of the stories in the current collection draw inspiration from these travels. "In the Mountains" and "Kol Nidre in the Music Hall" depict the milieu of semi-assimilated bohemian Jewish artists, intellectuals and vaudeville performers in Germany and Switzerland. Three short sketches, narrated by a Nomberg-like first person narrator, observe the life of boarding houses and hiking trails and the Jewish and non-Jewish tourists and wanderers to be

---

1 For a discussion of the Hebrew counterpart to "A Cheerful Soul" see Shachar Pinsker's article "Warsaw in Hebrew Literature 1880-1920: New Perspectives" in *Studia Judaica* 18 (2015), 133.

found there. The two final stories take place in Berlin after the First World War, exploring the trauma and nostalgia of refugees and permanent immigrants.

In all Nomberg wrote about fifty short stories, ranging from fully fleshed out narratives to short atmospheric sketches and creepy fairy tales.

When Nomberg's youngest son, Yekheskl, died of tuberculosis at the age of seventeen, Nomberg felt partly responsible: he blamed himself for not being able to afford the best doctors and that perhaps if things had been different the boy might have survived. This may be one of the reasons his fiction writing became less frequent and he concentrated his efforts on more lucrative journalistic work after the First World War.

Warsaw would remain his base for the rest of his life, but—in the words of his friend and fellow writer Froyim Kaganovski—Nomberg was always running away. He never settled at any one address. He moved apartments often and preferred to stay in hotels when he could. He often chose to stay in the non-Jewish side of town (such as when his housemates were a band of circus performers and professional wrestlers) and whenever he did have a fixed abode he would use it to store his obsessively collected gadgets, which he brought back from his frequent trips abroad—such as cameras, new-fangled shaving devices, and strange toothbrushes. He also developed a taste for good coffee—something he could not find in Warsaw—and it's said that, instead of going home after a night on the town, he would sometimes catch the night train to Berlin, waking up there in time for breakfast and a cup of coffee.

While Nomberg's fictional inspiration began to dry up, his regular columns and travel writing from North and South America, Palestine, and the Soviet Union only increased in popularity. He had a short lived career as a politician, but a life-long involvement in Yiddish cultural work. He served in the Sejm, the Polish parliament, on the ticket of the *Folkspartay*, a party dedicated to safeguarding secular Jewish cultural autonomy within the new Polish Republic. But more productively he was involved in the founding of the Union of Jewish Writers and Journalists, which became the new center for Jewish literary life in the city, if not the world. He was also involved in the newly established Yiddish language secular school movement. In those days—unlike today—translation was a lucrative side-gig for Yiddish writers and Nomberg translated drama from German and English—he boasted of being able to translate a Gerhardt Hauptmann play over the course of an afternoon or two. Nomberg translated a number of texts with an Orientalist flavor, including a well-regarded Yiddish versions of the *Thousand and One Nights*, as well as a collection of poetry by Nobel Prize winning Bengali Poet Rabindranath Tagore (translated from Tagore's own English version) and selected poems by Hafez, the fourteenth century Persian poet and mystic (adapted from the German translation by G.F. Daumer).[1]

Towards the end of the 1920s Nomberg's health deteriorated further and he had problems walking, though this did little to slow down his hectic nightlife until one night in 1927, while leaving the Writers' Union he collapsed on the stairs. He was taken to a sanatorium in Otwock and died soon thereafter. Despite being considered an old man of Yiddish letters, he was only fifty-one.

Daniel Kennedy,
Tours, August 2020

---

1 Zalman Reyzen, *Leksikon fun der yidisher literatur prese un filologye, vol 4* (Vilna: Farlag B. Kletskin, 1929), 807–820.

Glossary

Badkhn:
Wedding jester, an improviser of humorous and sentimental rhymes.

Daytshmerish:
A term for Yiddish speech or writing that is peppered with Germanisms. The popular Yiddish press often used a *daytshmerish* style (ridiculed in Yiddish literary circles) in writing, while in speech it was used in an attempt to cultivate an air of worldly sophistication.

Denikin:
Anton Ivanovich Denikin (1872–1947) was one of the founding members of the anti-Bolshevik Volunteer Army in Southern

Russia. Pogroms were carried out by various factions during the Russian Civil War, where an estimated 50,000 Jews perished.

Gnädiges Fräulein, Gnädiger Herr:
Formal German salutation: (lit:"Gracious")

Gymnasium: In central and Eastern Europe a secondary school generally preparing students to go on to university.

Goy (pl. goyim):
Non-Jew, Gentile.

Hasidism/Hasid: (Yid. *Khasidizm* or *khsides, khosid*)
A branch of orthodox Judaism originating in the eighteenth century which rapidly gained popularity throughout Eastern Europe. The opponents of Hasidism were known as the misnagdim. The central characteristics of Hasidism include allegiance to a particular Rebbe, or spiritual leader, emphasis on indi-

vidual prayer, and joyous worship involving singing, and dancing.

Kitl:
Long white linen coat worn by men on solemn holidays.

Kol Nidre:
An Aramaic declaration recited (or sung) in the synagogue before the beginning of the evening service on Yom Kippur. The melody associated with Kol Nidre in the Ashkenazi tradition is famously haunting and emotionally charged.

Kugel:
A pudding made of noodles, potatoes or bread, eaten traditionally on Shabbes midday. The comedian in "Kol Nidre at the Music Hall" drops many Yiddishisms into his speech for comic effect for the amusement of his assimilated Jewish audience who no doubt understand a few half-remembered Yiddish words.

Lithuania: (Yid. *Lite*)
Here, an area much larger than the modern state of Lithuania. Homeland of the Litvaks, a group whose regional identity is considerably older and more stable than the borders of Eastern Europe, living in the area roughly equivalent to modern-day Lithuania, Latvia, Belarus and parts of north-east Poland. The Litvaks differed from the *Poylish* (Polish) Jews and *Galitsyaner* (Galician/Ukrainian) Jews in their dialect, cuisine, and temperament.

Nikolayevsky Soldier:
Jews drafted into Russian military service from 1827 to 1856. Named for Nicholas I (1825–1855) whose *Ustav rekrutskoi povinnosti* (Statute on Conscription Duty) marked the beginning of compulsory military service for Jewish males over the age of 18. Military service lasted a staggering 25 years after which many Jews had all but abandoned much of their Jewish identity. The father in "Ishmael

is my Uncle" speaks a Yiddish peppered with Russian words and interjections (such as "*Panimayete?*" "You understand?" and "*Nye Pravda li?*" "Is that not so?" etc.)

Pan/Panie/Pani/Panna:
Polish honorifics were widely used in Yiddish. Pan (lit: sir) is the equivalent of Mr. (Panie, the vocative form is used when addressing a man directly) Pani is the equivalent of Mrs., while Panna, largely outdated in modern Polish, was the equivalent of Miss.

Peyes:
Side-locks worn by orthodox Jewish males.

Pogromchik: (Russian/Yiddish)
An instigator of or participant in a pogrom, an organized (often state sanctioned) massacre of Jews. Berlin in the 1920s was home to large number of Jewish refugees fleeing the pogroms in Russia as well as former anti-Bolshevik forces in hiding after their defeat.

The trope of Jewish refugee encountering a pogromchik in Berlin is one that would later be taken up by Dovid Bergelson in his 1928 story "Among Refugees" (available in Joachim Neugroschel's translation in *The Shadows of Berlin*, City Lights Books) inspired by the story of Sholem Schwartzbard who was tried for the murder of Symon Petliura, the commander of Ukrainian forces.

***The Political Economy*:**
Considering Toybkop's Socialist leanings, the work in question is probably *A Contribution to the Critique of Political Economy* by Karl Marx, (1859).

Reb:
Yiddish honorific, equivalent to Mr. Used with full name, or first name only.

Rebbe:
In Hasidism, the spiritual leader of a Hasidic dynasty. A mentor/teacher/spiritual guide more generally.

Sadigura
A Hasidic dynasty named for the city of Sadhora (Sadigura in Yiddish), Bukovina, Austro-Hungary.

Seder: (Yid. *Seyder*)
Holiday meal to mark Passover, celebrated as a family. The meal involves the eating of Matzah, ritual foods and the reading of the Haggadah.

Shabbes:
The Jewish Sabbath, beginning at sundown on Friday evening and ending on Saturday evening at dusk. Traditionally observant Jews are forbidden from all forms of work on Shabbes, including handling money, writing, traveling or making fire.

Sholem aleykhem, Aleykhem Sholem:
Traditional Yiddish greeting.

Shofar: (Yid. *Shoyfer*)
Ancient musical instrument made from a ram's horn. The Shofar is blown during synagogue services on Rosh Hashanah (*rosheshone*) and at the end of Yom Kippur (*yom kiper*). It is also blown every weekday morning during the month of Elul (*elel*) on the run-up to Rosh Hashanah.

Shoykhet:
A ritual slaughterer.

Shtreimel: (Yid. *Shtrayml*)
A round fur hat worn by many married Hasidim on Shabbes and religious holidays.

Tallis: (Yid. *tales*) or Tallit
A fringed prayer-shawl. Worn during morning prayer.

Wrangel, General:
Pyotr Wrangel (1878–1928) was commanding general of the anti-Bolshevik White Army during the Russian Civil War.

Yeshiva: (Yid. *yeshive*)
A school focused on the study of religious texts, particularly the Talmud and Torah. *Yeshive bokherim* were adolescent boys who had shown enough intellectual promise to warrant further study. Yeshivas were usually boarding-schools, with students often having to leave home and travel some distance to study there. Meals for poorer students were often provided on a charitable basis by nearby families.

Yom Kippur: (Yid. *Yom kiper*)
The Day of Atonement, the holiest day in the Jewish Year. Marked by a day of fasting, intensive prayer, and synagogue attendance.

A PARTIAL LIST OF SNUGGLY BOOKS

G. ALBERT AURIER *Elsewhere and Other Stories*
CHARLES BARBARA *My Lunatic Asylum*
S. HENRY BERTHOUD *Misanthropic Tales*
LÉON BLOY *The Desperate Man*
ÉLÉMIR BOURGES *The Twilight of the Gods*
CYRIEL BUYSSE *The Aunts*
FÉLICIEN CHAMPSAUR *The Latin Orgy*
BRENDAN CONNELL *Unofficial History of Pi Wei*
RAFAELA CONTRERAS *The Turquoise Ring and Other Stories*
ADOLFO COUVE *When I Think of My Missing Head*
LADY DILKE *The Outcast Spirit and Other Stories*
ÉDOUARD DUJARDIN *Hauntings*
ERCKMANN-CHATRIAN *A Malediction*
ALPHONSE ESQUIROS *The Enchanted Castle*
ENRIQUE GÓMEZ CARRILLO *Sentimental Stories*
EDMOND AND JULES DE GONCOURT *Manette Salomon*
REMY DE GOURMONT *From a Faraway Land*
GUIDO GOZZANO *Alcina and Other Stories*
GUSTAVE GUICHES *The Modesty of Sodom*
EDWARD HERON-ALLEN *The Complete Shorter Fiction*
J.-K. HUYSMANS *The Crowds of Lourdes*
JEAN LORRAIN *The Soul-Drinker and Other Decadent Fantasies*
ARTHUR MACHEN *Ornaments in Jade*
CAMILLE MAUCLAIR *The Frail Soul and Other Stories*
CATULLE MENDÈS *Mephistophela*
ÉPHRAÏM MIKHAËL *Halyartes and Other Poems in Prose*
LUIS DE MIRANDA *Who Killed the Poet?*
OCTAVE MIRBEAU *The Death of Balzac*
LÉO TRÉZENIK *Decadent Prose Pieces*
RUGGERO VASARI *Raun*
JANE DE LA VAUDÈRE *The Witch of Ecbatana and The Virgin of Israel*

CPSIA information can be obtained
at www.ICGtesting.com
Printed in the USA
BVHW031045130621
609463BV00007B/594